Operation Nightfall

Campfire Tales, Book 1

Robert E. Hampson

Brain and Brain Ink

Contents

Dedication

Operation Nightfall, a/k/a "On a Starry Night," is dedicated to the many Boy Scout leaders who shaped my youth, and the trainers and colleagues who assisted me as an adult leader. This story is a tribute to the Time Machine stories by Donald and Keith Monroe ("Donald Keith") that appeared in Boy's Life from 1959 to 1989. They might even be to blame for me growing up to write SF!

...and as always, for Ruann, the love of my life; for Mom, my first fan; and for Dad, my hero and role model.

Additional Copyright Information

OPERATION NIGHTFALL

Authors note: On A Starry Night *was originally written in 2014 as a stand-alone novella, but plans to publish a series of "Campfire Tales" fell through. When I first read Kevin Steverson's book* Salvage Title, *I was struck by how the characters reminded me of the old Boy's Life tales from my youth. The stories emphasized curiosity, ingenuity, self-sufficiency, and an overall positive view of the world. I sent* On a Starry Night *to Kevin, and he liked it, and with a few tweaks to make it fit the universe (as a sort of prequel), he included it in the novella collection* The Long and the Short of It.

This version has removed the Salvage Title-*specific references and is renamed to fit the events of the original story.*

"I've always loved a starry night," S.C. Davis told his Astronomy class. "On a clear night like tonight, you can see more stars than you could possibly see in the city. Even in orbit, on Luna or on Mars, you never get quite the same effect looking out through a dome or porthole as you get looking up at the stars in the wide-open sky. It's amazing how you look up and wish you were up there, but you get up there and find yourself wishing you were down here." The campfire had burned down to just a few embers, and the glow was just enough to see the handful of boys in the class. "When I was at camp, this class was always my favorite. Sitting around a campfire way past Taps, waiting for all of the lights to go out, hiking around in the dark, and staring at the summer sky all night. You know, I signed up for Astronomy three summers in a row!"

The boys gathered around the campfire laughed. They had a fresh, eager look that took Davis back to his own youth at this very same camp. The night air was cool, the sky was free of clouds, and the glowing embers were too dim to interfere with the distant light from the stars above. "Okay, look right up there, at the backwards question mark. Who can tell me the name of that constellation? Yes, Ben?"

"Is that Taurus?" asked one of the boys.

"No, Taurus is a winter constellation, not summer. I do like the winter sky—bold Orion, facing Taurus the Bull with the grand sweep of the Milky Way behind him. Perseus, Pisces, Pegasus; the glitter of the Pleiades, the bright glow of Sirius, Antares, and Betelgeuse. Some are of the opinion that the easiest constellations to identify are in the winter sky, but that won't help us now. It's July and those constellations have set. Tim?"

"That's Scorpio, right, Mr. Davis?"

"That's right, Tim. The 'T' shape is the head and claws of the scorpion. The sideways question mark is the tail stretching off to the left—that's east, Jake." The other boys laughed at Jakob as they watched him try to figure out the direction without shining a flashlight on his compass. "Okay, right over there." Davis aimed his laser pointer, and the fine line of green light reached out into the sky. "Looks like a 'W'. Anyone?"

"Cassiopeia, Mr. D.?"

"Yes, very good, Jordan. It is indeed Cassiopeia. If you look from there back to the Big Dipper, you can see the North Star. Now, who can point out Mars?"

"What's that, Mr. Davis?" Jordan interrupted, pointing to a glowing streak off to the west.

"A shooting star, most likely. Or, to use the scientific term, a meteor."

"Maybe it's a satellite!"

"Aliens invading, that's what it is!"

The boys were laughing and offering up their own silly interpretations of the streak of light in the night sky. "It could be a ship returning to Earth, right, Mr. Davis?"

Darkness hid his smile at a bittersweet memory. "Actually, Ben, you're right. It could be a ship coming back from Mars, the asteroid mines, or even the outer colonies." Davis poked at the fire with the tip of his cane and made a distinct 'thump' as he tapped the cane against his leg to knock the clinging embers from it. He reached across with his good hand to place another log and rekindle the flame. "But the chances are it's probably just a meteor. There are considerably more of them than there are spaceships in transit."

There was a general mumble of agreement from the boys as they admitted the odds favored the meteor. Unseen by them, however, was the sly smile playing across Davis' face. "On the other hand, boys, nights like tonight were made for campfire tales... and such tales always begin on a starry night. Let's add a bit more wood to the fire, there are some marshmallows in the pack over there." Davis stirred the embers and added a few small sticks to start a low flame burning.

"Speaking of spaceships, it was a clear night sky not unlike this one, many years ago in this very camp, when I looked up and saw what I thought was a meteor. I was a student counselor then, just a few years older than you guys."

The astronomy class met in the amphitheater where the stone benches and walls blocked the lights from the rest of camp. Since the theater stood on the lakefront, there was a clear view of most of the sky. To get a better view, they'd have to sit at the top of the local hill known as The Knob, and given that the rising full moon was presently behind the Knob, the view from the hilltop would actually have been worse for the purposes of the class.

The six boys and four girls were pretty excited about being away from their campsites after Lights Out, let alone finding themselves out in the darkness without flashlights or lanterns. Taps had been played more than half an hour ago and the only other boys permitted out this late were mucking about in the muddy reeds in search of frogs for their Reptiles and Amphibians class. The counselor had dialed a red filter over his light to dim it. He didn't really need it to check the requirements book—after all, it was on a tablet with its own illumination—but he had to see to figure out *where* he'd left the tablet. "Okay, guys, who can name three stars that we can see right now?" There was a shuffling and rustling sound as several hands went up. "Um, ladies and gentlemen, I appreciate you being polite, but I would remind you that no one can see your hand in the dark." The hands went down amid rueful chuckles.

"Mr. Davis?"

Skip Davis grimaced. He hated being addressed as 'Mister' but it was a camp rule for all counselors. "You'll have to tell me your name," he prompted the unknown speaker. "I'm afraid I don't recognize all your voices."

"It's Isaac, sir. I can name three stars."

Sir. Skip wanted to sigh, although he could hardly fault the boy for being properly raised, but he supposed it was due to the close quarters where he lived. Being called 'sir' made him feel old, although at twenty-four he supposed he was probably a full-fledged grownup in their teenage eyes. "Go ahead, Isaac. The rest of you listen and see if you can come up with some more names."

"Okay, so right up there is Altair." Isaac pointed to the head of a constellation that looked vaguely like a kite. "Those other two bright stars are Deneb and Vega."

Skip was impressed. "Very good, we don't get too many guys from the conurbs who know their stars, let alone the Summer Triangle. Well done, Isaac."

He put down his light and tablet and reached into his pocket for the green laser pointer he used to point out constellations. Before turning it on, he looked carefully at the sky for any moving lights and listened for the sound of aircraft engines—it was worse than a bad idea to shine the bright light of a laser near an aircraft cockpit, it was illegal. "Okay, gentlemen, ladies." The group giggled. Skip merely waited for it to die down. "As I was saying, let's find the constellations where those stars are found." He pressed the button to activate the laser, careful to keep it pointed up towards the sky, and traced a cross shape against the stars.

"This is Cygnus, the Swan, with Deneb at its head." Next was the kite shape. "This is Aquila, the Eagle, and right there is Deneb again. You really can't see much of Lyra, but it looks like a miniature kite with Vega at the tail." Davis traced the triangle of the three bright stars. "We call them the 'Summer Triangle' since they are the three brightest stars in the summer sky, and some of the most easily found, as they are located nearly straight over our heads."

Skip smiled to himself as he listened to the kids, one by one, spot the stars he'd indicated. This was what he loved to do more than anything else. Looking up at the night sky—whether teaching astronomy or simply sitting alone and staring at the stars—always filled him with wonder and fueled his imagination. Well, more than *almost* anything else, he corrected himself. There was something to be said for reading a good book, preferably one by Heinlein or Asimov, in front of a winter fire, but it was the night sky that inspired his dreams. He was fortunate indeed that the U.S. had decided that some areas *needed* to be protected from the encroachment of the cities.

"So, what's that bright one over there?" asked one of the girls, unidentifiable in the dark. "The orangey one."

"That's Mars, you idiot!" That triggered a chorus of titters and jeers from the other kids.

"I don't think that's Mars. I mean, it's growing brighter!"

Skip couldn't see where the girl was pointing. "It's probably just a meteor," he said as he turned to look to the west.

And then he saw the orange object. It was indeed growing brighter. It was moving, too, moving fast, and it looked as if it was headed right towards them. As it rapidly grew larger, the kids began to scramble for the nearest cover. Only Skip stood there, watching in frozen astonishment as the bright orange light streaked by overhead and disappeared beyond the wall of the amphitheater, followed by a searing roar like a jet fighter or a rocket. Moments later, there was a strange sound like tearing cloth, followed by a gigantic boom that made all of them jump.

The object had disappeared behind The Knob. Had it crashed to Earth? There was the slightest orange glow coming from that direction. Between the ringing in his ears and the nervous shouts of alarm and fear and excitement, it was hard for Skip to hear the frantic calls that started to come in on his radio handset. He dialed the red filter off his hand lamp and dialed up the illumination to get a good look at his group. Most of the boys and a couple of the girls were grinning and wide-eyed with excitement, but a few were visibly upset. Skip couldn't blame them. He was pretty shaken himself. Because, just for a moment, he thought he'd seen something as the object passed by overhead. When he'd turned around, with his laser pointer still directed skyward, he thought he'd seen an unexpected reflection, as if some sort of shiny surface had bounced the green light back toward the ground.

An authoritative voice on the radio finally cut through the gabbling chaos, demanding order and discipline. It was Mr. Keith, the Campmaster. "Davis. Davis! You there?" He assigned the counselors' schedules, and he could track their location through the camp-issued communicators, so he was quite aware that Skip and his astronomy class were still outside. "Talk to me, S.C.!"

"I'm here, sir. I've got my class at the arena. Everyone is all right. Just a little more excitement than we bargained for." Skip kept his voice level, knowing the boys and girls needed him to remain calm. "Sir, I think the first thing we should do is get them buddied up and back to their tents and cabins. However, I have three singletons from separate sites."

"Glad to hear it. That sounds like a good plan, Davis. I'm on my way there, so stay put. I'll send staff to escort the three individual boys back to their campsites. Do you want to send the others back now? Or wait for a runabout?"

"Let me do a check—guys! Flashlight check! One, two, three... No, Jacob, Night vision glasses don't count. Okay, I have ten campers with nine flashlights. Now... Buddy check?" There was a group of two boys, three boys, two girls, and one boy and two girls by themselves. "Alright, sir, I can send two groups of boys back by themselves. There's a group of two and a group of three from the same or adjacent campsites. I have one buddy pair of females, two singles, and a single male. I'm sending the buddy groups on back, and we'll wait on the runabout for the rest."

"Good. Tell those boys heading back to the larger sites to have an adult leader call the camp office when they get back, S.C. There'll be a general meeting later after everyone gets back."

"Understood, sir. I'll keep the girls and the one boy with me until the runabout arrives." Skip put the radio back on his belt and turned back to the boys. "Okay, Jordan! You're the oldest, so take the two boys from your unit and head back with them. James and Emery, you go with Jordan too, since they'll pass your site on the way. You heard Mr. Keith: tell one of your leaders to report in once you get back so no one has to go out looking for you. Jordan, remind James and Emery– no, better yet, just tell their leader yourself. Louis and Frank, head back to your site now. Do the same, have an adult call in upon arrival. Suki and Sara, I know you're buddied up, but your leader wouldn't want you heading back alone. There'll be a female staffer coming to give you all a lift back. Isaac, Kaylee, and Zoe, you're staying with me. Now, the rest of you. Flashlights on, watch the ground, and stay together!"

Skip watched the boys walk away, flashlights carefully sweeping the ground back and forth as they'd been taught. He motioned to the remaining kids to have a seat on the benches. Units were advised that they should try to have at least two kids take each night class so they could buddy up and travel together, but sometimes a unit was too small or didn't have two younger Scouts to take the class. Skip usually walked the single boys back to their sites himself and called on his friend and fellow staff member, Claire, to walk the girls back. Under the unusual circumstances tonight, others would have to do it. Mr. Keith was already on his way to the amphitheater, and Skip had a pretty good idea why.

A few minutes later, a two-seat electric cart pulled up, and the campmaster stepped off. Right behind him was an eight-seat ground-effect runabout—one of two in the camp, usually used for medical transport. Two of the senior counselors, one male, one female, were up front. Skip noted that Claire was driving. Mr. Keith directed the five remaining Scouts to get on the runabout. Once safely loaded, Claire called their leaders on the headset radio she wore when driving. Once she had checked on everyone's destination, they headed back down the hard-packed dirt road leading back toward the campsites.

Mr. Keith was the oldest of the permanent staff, and the boys knew him as 'Mister Keith' or 'Campmaster.' One had to become a counselor before learning that Keith was actually his first name. Keith Rogers had been an employee of the camp since before many of the current counselors were born, and he lived most of the year in a house just a quarter mile outside the main gate. Despite his age, he was still active, and most of the staffers had trouble keeping up with him.

Skip had gotten out his navpak compass/GPS handheld while the others had been loading onto the runabout, and he was making notes on his tablet. The campmaster looked curious, but he held his tongue and did not interfere until he was finished. "So, everyone's been complaining about the light and noise, Davis, but no one else seems to have seen it. But if you were doing what you were supposed to be doing and staring at the sky, I reckon you and your class must have seen something. Was it a flyer?"

Skip slipped his stylus and the compass back into his jacket. "Well, sir, it really looked like a meteor at first, but as it passed overhead, I thought I saw it deflect my pointer. And while I wouldn't swear to it, I thought I saw some sort of triangular shape."

Keith nodded. "I'm worried it may have been an aircraft crashing. It's been a dry spring and summer, if there was a crash and a fire started, we could have a real problem on our hands. We need to get on this right away. So, what have you got there?" He pointed to the tablet in Skip's hand.

Skip handed it to him and adjusted the backlight so the campmaster had enough light to see the rough sketch of the amphitheater wall, marked with an Indian mask and a straight line overhead. "I mentioned the laser pointer." Davis clicked on the laser and a thin green beam could be seen shining straight up as it reflected off dust and residual campfire smoke still drifting through the camp. "If you could move just a bit to the right," Davis directed, careful to avoid shining the laser in his eyes. He twisted his wrist and moved the beam down until it intersected the amphitheater wall behind a row of seats. "I remember very clearly seeing that Akela mask over there in the glow, and the line of the reflected laser was about a foot to the right."

He stepped out into the middle of the grass to a small stone pedestal. "I always place my star maps for the class on this pedestal, so I know I was standing here." Davis pulled out his compass and held it up to align the fluorescent markings on the dial. "That's ninety true to the mask, and I'd estimate another two degrees to the right, which gives us 92 degrees."

The campmaster reached out his hand, and Skip handed over the navpak. Keith tapped and pressed on the touch screen for a few moments, then turned the screen to show the others. "So, just north of the Knob, then. Good. That gives us a starting point. How high overhead would you guess it was?"

"The Knob's seven hundred meters, the lake's around three twenty, so the peak of the Knob is about three hundred eighty meters above us." Skip thought a moment. "It's just a guess, but I'd call it about three times the height of the Knob. Close to a thousand meters."

"Good eyes, Davis. I knew I could count on you to have noticed something. We can work with this." He handed back the navpak and headed over to his cart. "Okay, Davis. Let's confirm that your class got back safe and then we'll meet in the dining hall at... " He looked at his wristcomp. "Twenty-three hundred. I'm headed back there now—want a ride?"

"No, thank you sir, I'll walk. I need to stop by my quarters anyway."

"Fine. Just be there at twenty-three hundred. So, what do you think? Do you think you can track where it went?"

"Yes, sir. I think so. Whatever it was, it went straight over the Knob in the direction of Hedgehog Mountain." A thought occurred to him. "Umm, sir, if you're worried about fire, shouldn't someone go out to the backside of the Knob tonight?"

"Someone will. Not necessarily us. We'll see. Since you're headed past your quarters, perhaps you'd like to grab your gear?"

"Yes, sir!" He nodded eagerly and set off at once. He had about thirty minutes. It was a ten-minute hike to his quarters, then another eight to reach the dining hall. He'd have to leg it if he was going to make it there on time.

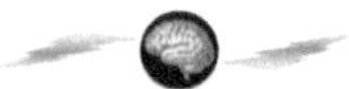

Eight minutes later, Skip was panting from his high-speed uphill hike as he threw open the door of his bunkroom. One of the privileges of being over eighteen and a returning counselor was being assigned one of the semiprivate rooms in the bunkhouse. It was larger than his first college dorm room, but smaller than his current apartment. He was nominally sharing it, but for the moment, he had it all to himself since his roommate was off at national training school, in preparation for becoming a member of the camp's permanent staff. Normally tidy, Skip had allowed a bit of clutter to accumulate, most of which was piled on his absent roommate's bunk. The impromptu shelf held textbooks, camping supplies and first aid components. He'd have to straighten it all out before Ronald returned. He ticked off the items he thought he might need. "Let's see, aid bag, staff, maybe a bigger knife or a tomahawk? Hmmm. Power cells... batteries, batteries, batteries..." He continued searching for the compact electrical storage units that were more than simply batteries; at the same time, he started placing items in a backpack. The final item looked like a cross between a flashlight and a satellite antenna, and it barely fit on the top, and he had to tie down the flap that closed and sealed the pack.

"Ah, there you are!" He inserted the spare power cells in a side pocket, slipped the pack over his shoulders, slid a carved wooden staff in the loops on the side, then grabbed a compact First Responder's pack, mostly consisting of a handheld field autodoc plus various bandaging supplies. He checked his watch and saw that he had less than ten minutes to make it to the meeting. That made the next decision easy. He needed to move fast, and there would probably be a need for a vehicle that could handle the "outback" terrain of the less commonly traveled areas of camp. Opening a desk drawer, he withdrew the keys to his jeep, spun the ring on his finger a few times, and headed out back to the parking area.

It was late, and he would be passing campsites, so Skip had to keep his speed down. It was almost twenty-three hundred when he pulled up in front of the dining hall. It could hold just under a thousand people at full capacity, but tonight there were only fifty staff members and a similar number of adult leaders from the forty-some troops in camp this week.

Keith had the public address microphone in hand. "Okay, people, listen up. We have no idea what produced that little show tonight. Davis, here, one of our counselors, was the only one to see it. It could have been a meteorite, could have been lightning, it might have been some sort of aircraft. He saw it disappear behind the Knob. *If* it was a flyer, and *if* it crashed, we need to know that *before* we wake up to a wildfire coming over the ridge. Also, if it was a crash, there may be a pilot or passenger in need of assistance. Either way, we need to investigate. Nine-one-one says nobody around the dispatch center saw anything, although they did get a few calls from around the county, so it looks like it may have come in right over the camp. I've been in touch with the sheriff as well; he's sending a search team over. He can send a flitter to look past the Knob, but not until daylight. I'm sure you can all guess his instructions." Keith affected a hill-country drawl. "'Y'all are not, repeat, not going looking for whatever-the-hell that thing was! I don't want any Boy Scouts nosing around my crash site!'"

A disrespectful murmur arose from the assembled group. "No, no. The sheriff's right! It's our land all right, but he has the final say on the county's emergency procedures. So, until daylight comes, and we get the sheriff's approval, we are not going to mobilize any search teams. However, we know the area, and they don't. So, I am detailing a small group to meet the sheriff's team and serve as guides."

The campmaster unrolled a large map of electrostatic "smart paper" on the closest table. He tapped his phone, and the sheet displayed a topographic map of the camp. He called Skip over and asked him to draw the estimated course of the object. The counselor pulled out his navpak and transferred the calculations from earlier that evening. Most of those present crowded around the table, but only a few could see the map. His part done for the moment; Skip stepped back so others could examine it.

The map showed a dashed red line extending from the amphitheater, aimed directly at a ridge five miles past the Knob labeled 'Hedgehog Mountain'. Campsites and facilities only occupied a fraction of the camp's property. The prospective landing zone was well within the camp boundaries, but there were no roads, and few trails in the area marked on the map as 'Beaver Creek Wilderness Campground'—more commonly known in camp as 'The Outback.'

One man ignored the map and approached him instead: "How high was it, son?" Upon hearing an estimate of one thousand meters, he grunted. "Okay, if it's suborbital ballistic—a meteorite, that is—it would be coming in at a descent angle of around twenty degrees, so your mysterious object should be on the ground about three thousand meters from where you saw it pass overhead. If it's much further out than that, you can be pretty sure it wasn't just falling."

Skip looked up at the speaker but didn't recognize him beyond a faint recollection of having seen him around the camp before. The man was clearly amused at Skip's puzzlement and extended his hand. "I'm Donnie. I know aircraft pretty well—I'm a pilot and a flight instructor. I suppose I might be useful if there was actually a crash, God forbid."

"I was going to ask for a volunteer to come along with Davis and me," Keith said, having overheard Donnie. You in, Captain?" At Donnie's nod, he continued. "Under most circumstances, I would send two volunteers along with one of the permanent staff, but seeing as how it's the sheriff involved, I'd better go myself."

He raised his voice and addressed the hall. "All right, now you know what's going on. I'll be out with the sheriff's team and will keep you posted. These two will accompany me; the rest of you get back to camp and bunks. Settle your campers, then hit the rack. If we have to alert the camp for some reason, you'll want as much rest as you can get. We'll have a full camp assembly out front at oh seven hundred. Leaders at oh six thirty."

They wouldn't get much sleep, Skip thought, although more than he would. He glanced at Donnie. Captain? Captain of what? Air Force, maybe? His hair was short enough to be military, and the man did hold himself with the straight-backed vigilance of other military men Skip had known.

As the group dispersed, Keith looked at Skip. "I heard your jeep. Mind if I drive? It'll look better than showing up in a golf cart!" Skip didn't mind, and handed over the keys. The sheriff and the campmaster never quite got along, and all of the staff knew it. The camp was firmly in the Blue Ridge Protected Zone and was technically under the jurisdiction of the Wilderness Preservation Conservancy, moreover, the camp was designated a historic site and had the hundred-year-old documents to prove it. The sheriff was responsible for the county, though, and given that those charter documents were originally with the state and county, he had jurisdiction.

Sheriff Hixson wasn't keen on the city and arcology kids that came to camp and often reminded Keith that the county had enough rural hoodlums without importing the urban variety. He also let it be known that he didn't like city folk who moved to the countryside and brought their city habits with them. Skip had heard that last part because the parents of one of his good friends had moved up from Char-Salem and had a few run-ins with Hixson's deputies.

As they opened the doors of the jeep, Keith pointed at the collection of gear Skip had assembled and smiled. "I see you still take the motto seriously. You remind me of your Uncle Bill. I suspect he always thought there was a silent 'for all eventualities' after 'be prepared'."

"Is that a satcomm, ion cannon or just a really big flashlight?" Donnie pointed to the oversized dish device sticking out of the top of the pack.

"Sometimes you need to see where you're going, sir. My uncle, that's the same Uncle Bill that Mr. Keith knows, he once told me that when you do a real live rescue, the one thing you're usually missing is light."

"Call me Donnie, son."

"Yessir."

Keith started the car and laughed. "Well, S.C., Bill Davis would certainly know. He probably told you about the time he, your father and I had to pull a camper out of a cave on a night like this when all we had were helmet lanterns."

"Yessir, it's one of his favorite stories."

"Ah, but did he ever tell you the camper was your mom?"

By the time the sheriff and his team called twenty minutes later, it was well after midnight, and Skip was starting to feel the effects of a long day. He'd worked the nighttime shift at the health lodge, the breakfast serving line, a full day of events, demonstrations, meetings, and games, and then taught the evening astronomy class. It turned out that both Keith and Donnie were prepared for that. The captain distributed energy bars, saying he preferred them to coffee on long flights for obvious reasons. Keith, on the other hand, preferred coffee in all circumstances. He had topped off a thermos in the dining hall before they left. He offered some to Skip, who found it strong enough to make him blink. In company with the energy bar, it helped keep exhaustion at bay.

Three ground effect trucks full of men—including men in the open beds in violation of camp rules—were pulled up to the front gate of the camp. Sheriff Hixson was quick to let Keith know his displeasure that the entrance had not been left open for him. While the two conversed, Skip activated the control to retract the gate, then closed it again once the trucks had passed through. His need to demonstrate authority sated, the sheriff and his men began reviewing their own navpaks and tables without bothering to consult Skip or the other two men from the camp.

"So, what do they call you, son, besides Mister Davis?" There was not much for them to do at the moment. Keith had tried to show the sheriff the map Skip marked, but he was pointedly ignored.

"Here they mostly just call me Davis. My friends at school call me Skip, but the boys have to call me Mister."

"School?"

"Mr. Davis here, or S.C. as he is more commonly known among the staff, is in medical school," Keith said, grinning at a discomfited Skip.

"A doctor-to-be," Donnie said, nodding as if he was impressed. "Might come in handy if we have to break out that med kit. S.C. your initials?"

"No. Well, yes. Um, not entirely."

"No? Yes?" Donnie expression turned to one of amusement.

Keith laughed, and then clarified for Donnie. "It usually stands for Space Cadet. I suspect you can deduce the etymology seeing as how Mr. Davis here teaches astronomy, reads science fiction, and spends more time outside looking at the stars than he does cracking Gray's Anatomy. If you see him in the health lodge, he's either got a textbook reader in his hand or a star chart."

"Space Kay-det," said Donnie in an exaggerated drawl. He looked amused and stroked his chin. A faraway look came over his face for a moment but then he focused on Skip and spoke in his normal voice. "I've heard worse, son." Skip grimaced, but Donnie only smiled, punched him in the arm and said: "Just riding you, Skip. Keith, it looks like your sheriff's finally ready to move out. What say we take a little moonlight drive?"

"Not my sheriff," muttered Keith as he climbed behind the wheel. Donnie took shotgun, and Skip got into the back. They pulled into line behind the other vehicles. "I didn't vote for the son-of-a—whatever."

Sheriff Hixson insisted, at first, that his vehicle should lead, but when his truck almost ran off the winding trail twice in the darkness, he ordered the Jeep to take the lead. That was how Keith, Donnie and Skip reached Beaver Creek before anyone else. North and east of the Knob were several square miles of wilderness where units were allowed to hike, backpack and practice low-impact camping. The track they followed couldn't really be called a road—or even a trail—but the Jeep had little trouble with it thanks to its four-wheel drive. The trail wound around the side of the Knob, splashed down into Beaver Creek, then turned to follow the creek bed for about 50 meters before climbing out the other side...into what both Keith and Skip were astonished to see was a great, big trench that clearly hadn't been there before.

Keith stopped to allow Skip to clamp the floodlight to the roll bar of the jeep and connect it to one of the spare power cells. For full power, he'd have to hook it directly to the Jeep's electrical system, but this was still enough to light up a surprisingly large section of the valley. The trench was a long furrow of severely disturbed ground, extending from east to west over the Knob, and ending at side of the valley a couple hundred meters away, as if someone had been strip-mining the land. The ground that wasn't chewed up looked scorched, but nothing appeared to be burning now. The trench also seemed to get narrower toward the far end, but Skip thought it might merely be a trick of the eye due to the shadows cast by the bright artificial light.

Sheriff Hixson stopped his truck in front of the jeep, managing to block most of the light on the scene. He slid out of the driver's seat and took charge, ordering the camp staff to stay back near the edge of the creek until he had the first look. Followed by three of his men, he walked down to the trench and then began walking alongside it. One guy had something that looked like a metal detector and started waving it around. Apparently, it detected something, because an alarm sounded as the man waved it back and forth.

Keith and Donnie followed the sheriff's path down to the trench; Skip decided he should stay put until he heard otherwise and remained with the jeep. Donnie was studying the broken ground while Keith went up to Hixson, who waved him off impatiently. Donnie came back to the jeep and asked: "Got a shovel back there, Kay-det?" Skip dug around in the back of the jeep for a moment, before finding a compact shovel. He handed it to Donnie, then followed quietly behind the older man as he went back to the trench and walked down the center until he reached the very end. There, he started to dig as Skip shined the light on him. The sheriff started to protest, but Donnie turned and glared at him until the man shut up, then went back to digging. The hole had been dug a few feet deep when there was a sound from the shovel hitting a solid object. Donnie lifted the shovel to reveal a black, irregular object. It was radiating heat; you could feel it from several feet away.

"That's it, then. Meteorite," said Donnie, lifting it up with the shovel, then flipping the shovel over to dump it at the sheriff's feet. "Oh, and I wouldn't touch it without gloves just yet," he added as the sheriff bent over and reached for it. Hixson straightened up quickly and motioned to one of his men to deal with the rock.

"Can we have it for the astronomy class?" Davis asked.

"Perhaps eventually, but not yet," answered Keith. "I imagine there will be a few folks who will want to take a look at it first." The campmaster shared a glance with Donnie, who nodded. "Give it a few days and then I'll see if we can claim it." He shooed both Donnie and Skip back to the Jeep, told Skip to get behind the wheel, then unclipped his radio, leaving the sheriff to try to figure out what to do with the still-hot meteorite.

"Okay," said Keith when he finished a brief conversation and returned the radio to his belt. "Let's get the two of you back to camp. I've got to meet a water buffalo from the National Guard and see that they wet down this area properly. Donnie, you should get back to your boys. Davis, you need to get some rack time. By the way, the two of you are excused from the oh six thirty and oh seven hundred assemblies, but I'd like to see you both in the admin cabin around oh nine hundred. Drop me at the front gate, please, S.C., then you can head back to quarters."

The campmaster shouted a warning to the sheriff and others that he was turning off the light, so a few of the sheriff's men got out handheld flashlights as Keith switched it off. As Skip's eyes adjusted to the sudden dark, he thought he saw something past the end of the field as it gradually rose into the slopes of Hedgehog Mountain. It was yellow-orange and shimmering. But the light faded quickly, so he supposed it was just an aftereffect of the sudden darkness on his eyes.

"Can you switch that thing back on?" asked Donnie. "I thought I saw something."

"You, too?" asked Keith.

Skip added that he had seen it as well. Unfortunately, the intense heat of the illuminator source meant that it couldn't be switched off, then on again, without being allowed to cool. Keith and Skip directed their flashlights in that direction, and Skip turned on the Jeep's high beams, but even the combined light they produced were too weak to penetrate the darkness at such a distance.

There was nothing to see. The campmaster shrugged and told Skip to turn the vehicle around. The night would keep its secrets for now.

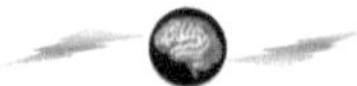

At precisely oh nine hundred, Skip walked into the campmaster's office. Donnie was already there and was even freshly shaven. Skip had pulled plenty of all-nighters before, so he wasn't surprised that the small amount of sleep he'd managed actually felt worse than none at all. Coffee was definitely in order, and fortunately, Mr. Keith had a pot brewing. It was the good stuff, too, none of the dining hall's instant crystals.

Even better, Mr. Keith had arranged to provide breakfast since he knew they'd be missing mess call: sausage biscuits from a local restaurant famous for them and an assortment of doughnuts. Skip's eyes narrowed in suspicion even as his belly growled with hunger. There was, he was entirely certain, another shoe to drop.

But Keith greeted them with an air of cheerful innocence: "Good morning, campers!" He smiled and gestured with his mug toward the coffee pot which, judging by the level, indicated he was already on his second cup. "Sheriff Hixson said there was nothing in the field except for the meteorite, but I do believe he's wrong."

"You think we *did* see something when the light went out!" Skip pressed him as he reached for a biscuit.

"Well, I too, think there was something there," Donnie jumped in. "I called someone I know at air traffic control this morning. He said the radar return on whatever it was last night was a lot bigger than that meteorite we pulled out of the dirt."

"The meteorite was about the size of a softball. Could it have hit a flyer, maybe? My pointer didn't bounce off that little thing."

"That would be extremely rare to such an extent that I've never heard of it happening. Actually, my friend suggested there might be some bigger pieces out there and that little meteorite was just a piece that fell off early when it hit the ground."

"But where would the rest of it be?" Keith asked.

"I have an idea," Skip said, reaching for the smart paper topo map they'd used last night. He pulled out a stylus and marked a line just off Beaver Creek. "This is the trench we saw." He tapped the line drawn the night before. "Along here."

"So, what are you thinking?" Donnie asked.

"Last night, I estimated the object was over a thousand meters up, based on Donnie calling a twenty-degree angle and it being high enough to clear the Knob. However, the beam on the star pointer is only good for two thousand meters on a warm humid night like last night. I clearly saw it reflect back to ground, so the height would have to be under a thousand meters. If the descent angle was less than 20% and it was that low, we were looking too close."

"Let's work from that," Keith decided. "So, here's the arena at 1142 feet elevation, that's 348 meters. The Knob is 2297 feet. Eleven hundred fifty feet and change vertical, plus thirty-five hundred feet horizontal distance. Conservatively figure the object at five hundred meters or a bit over fifteen hundred feet above Davis at the arena...to clear the Knob, it could drop no more than three hundred fifty feet in thirty-five hundred."

"That's a one-in-ten rate of descent," Donnie mused. Skip was trying to keep up with their switching back and forth between feet and meters. He was used to metric measures in his science classes, but it was clear that the two older men were more comfortable with the more colloquial measure. "Ten percent slope is not unusual for an aircraft. At twelve eighty-six feet, Beaver Creek is at the same elevation as most of the camp, and it's another four thousand feet behind the Knob. To clear the hilltop, but land here," he tapped the map, "required the object to drop another thousand feet. That's a one-in-four rate of descent. It doesn't add up."

"That's a change from ten percent descent to almost twenty-five percent. Five degrees to nearly fifteen degrees." Skip whistled. "You know, a ballistic fall could do that! There is just one problem."

"Meteors don't fall in a ballistic path," Donnie said, nodding at him with a look of measured approval.

Keith frowned. "I'll take your word for it. So where do we look? And what are we looking for?"

"Something that definitely isn't a meteor," Donnie said as he tapped a spot on the map. "And it's right around here. If the terrain were flat it would take nearly ten miles, but Hedgehog Mountain is in the way, and it's only five miles out. I'd call it five or six hundred feet up the side of the mountain."

The campmaster frowned. Then he shrugged. "At least we know it didn't start any fires. All right, S.C., you're off the staff rotation for the day. The fire chief expects me to go back out to the meteor site today with him, so you'll have to go without me. We already received the all clear from the sheriff, so there is no reason I can't send you two out to take a look. Set your radios to channel 30 or use your cell phones if you can get a signal there. You'll have to take the long way around the lake, up Ridge Road to the 'Hog. Can your jeep make that trail?"

"Yes sir, well, at least to the old log cabin here." Davis indicated a point on the map about a quarter mile from the target Donnie had identified. "We can hike from there. It shouldn't be too rough."

"Check it out and let me know what you find. Call the sheriff if there is an emergency, but whatever you find there, you call me first."

It only took half an hour to get everything together. Donnie returned to his campsite for his gear and to change into proper hiking boots. Skip went to the mess hall pantry and made sandwiches, filled up several canteens with water and a plastic bottle with bug repellent, then drove to pick up Donnie at his campsite. He had a map, but Donnie pulled his own navpak out of his backpack; it was much more complicated than Skip's compass-and-GPS unit. "This should help. Same brand as I use in a plane," he explained. "I loaded topo maps so we can follow it right to the most likely site."

Unsurprisingly, the navpak led them on the trail around the back side of the lake. The trail climbed about halfway up the Knob, back down across the lower end of Beaver Creek, then up along a ridge that led towards Hedgehog Mountain. It was a bumpy ride, but the old Jeep was able to take it, unlike a more modern ground effect vehicle. It was only five miles by flitter to the old log cabin, but the Jeep had to cover more than eight, as they wound their way around the hills.

Once they arrived at the cabin, Skip began unloading their gear out of the back of the Jeep. He grabbed a daypack with water, food, poncho, first aid kit, compass, bug spray, whistle, and other hiking supplies. He started attaching his usual around-the-camp items to his belt—pocketknife, camp radio, flashlight holster, and a satellite repeater for his wristcomp—ground-based wireless communications were useless in WPC Protected Zones. Finally, he pulled out the hiking stick he'd left in the vehicle the night before.

Donnie joined him at the rear and removed his own pack, a small daypack like Skip's. However, the next item he withdrew was strictly nonregulation.

"Ah, sir, sheathed knives are not allowed in camp."

"I'm sure they aren't. I didn't let Emery bring his to camp," Donnie said as he tied the bottom loop of a long scabbard to his thigh. "Besides, it's not really a knife. We'll be happy to have it if we have to cut brush on the way."

Skip didn't like to see the camp rules so casually broken, but the man was not a young camper, and besides, this was neither the time nor the place for an argument. He nodded as if he agreed and let the matter drop. For now.

Their destination was not on any of the usual trails. There was a small game path that led in the general direction they were headed, but it kept taking them below the destination marker on Donnie's navpak. To approach the target from up-slope, they were forced to climb two hundred feet up the mountainside without any sort of trail. Skip was soon glad that Donnie had thought to bring the machete. It was a rough trail, and it was nearly noon by the time they approached another area of scorched vegetation.

Donnie was leading the way, but when he stopped, he motioned for Skip to be quiet. Skip noticed Donnie's right hand slide towards the small of his back.

From that, Skip surmised that the older man was carrying something else against the rules. It made him anxious, although he wasn't sure if it was the possibility Donnie was carrying a gun or the idea that Donnie had good reason to think he might need a gun that concerned him more. Despite the scorched earth, there were no signs of fire at present. The scorching was more indicative of a lot of heat, very much like what they had seen last night in the valley below. The smell of hot vegetation in front of them was stronger than the scent of cut vegetation from behind. Listening carefully, Skip could hear the usual sounds of the outdoors, insects buzzing, birds chirping, the sighing of the wind, as well as a loud clank, a thud that sounded as if something had struck a large piece of plastic—and the sound of someone cursing!

If it was aliens, they had a surprisingly extensive human vocabulary. Donnie relaxed, smiled, stepped into the area cleared by the recent burn and called out in a loud voice: "Delta Sierra Sierra Charlie Foxtrot Xray five niner. Say again your status!"

There was a sound of something hitting plastic again, and the cursing started back up. "Dammit, Control! What do you think my status is? Talk about a Charlie Foxtrot!" There was the sound of someone moving around somewhere nearby. "I sure hope you brought some ibuprofen. That's the third time I've hit my head!"

Skip followed Donnie into the clearing. There he saw the object he'd barely glimpsed overhead the previous night. It looked, for all the world, like a black arrowhead. The surface wasn't exactly smooth, it was more like the matte black used to paint models of stealth aircraft. It looked quite a bit like an early stealth aircraft, but smaller, about twenty feet long and fifteen feet wide. There was a cockpit up top, but there was neither a tail nor proper wings, and where Skip expected to see exhaust nozzles for a jet engine in the back, there were huge orange lenses.

A-ha, he thought. That was what they had seen last night when the spotlight was switched off!

The aircraft—or was it a spacecraft?—appeared to be supported on two legs extending down from the two corners of the triangle, but the nose of the craft was tilted down and touching the ground. A man was crawling out from un-derneath. A very human man, although his vehicle didn't look like any human aircraft Skip had ever seen. However, Donnie appeared to know exactly what was going on, and somehow, even appeared to know the stranger. Even more incredibly, the pilot appeared to know Donnie!

"Emerson Donelly, you old..." He started cursing again.

Donnie held up his hand. "Lock it up, Mike, you're in amongst Boy Scouts. Watch your language."

"Boy Scouts? What are you doing here, Don? My comm's broken, I think my leg's broken, this heap of–" he glanced at Skip and paused judiciously. "Well, whatever it is, it won't fly, and I don't know where I am!"

"You're in my backyard is where you are. We can sort out the rest of it in time, but at least you're alive. Sorry about letting you spend the night in the wilds, but it couldn't be helped. There were too many locals about." He reached out and helped the man get out from under the craft and sit down on the hillside with his left leg awkwardly extended. Skip could see that he was indeed fully human. Mike was about six feet, with thinning brown hair and light skin. He was thin and lanky, and he wore a dark gray flight suit covered with soot, grease, and red dirt. And, Skip noticed, absolutely none of the usual insignia that adorned the Air Force or even Space Force flight suits.

"Kaydet, you have the honor of meeting Major Mike Lukasz." He pro-nounced it 'Loo-kash.' "We work together. Mike, this is Eagle Ridge Senior Camp Counselor Skip Davis. I'll vouch for him. Oh, and Skip, you needn't worry. Campmaster Rogers has a very good inkling of what's going on here. I filled him in this morning before we set out. But you have to understand, outside of the four of us, this did *not* happen, and you did *not* see this. Clear?"

Skip swallowed hard. If Donnie had been willing to leave the major out to die overnight rather than risk exposing whatever program this was to the sheriff, then he clearly wasn't kidding around. "Yes sir. I...I'll keep my mouth shut, sir. Promise."

"Good. Now, I know you're an Eagle Scout, and you take your word seriously, but this is really serious stuff. Are you willing to swear an oath on it? Because if you're willing, we can sure use your help. Understood?"

"Yessir! I do understand, and I'm willing to swear on my honor, if need be."

"All right, that's good enough for me." Donnie turned back to the pilot. "Mike, I got a text from DSS at oh dark thirty. They pinged everyone's GPS coordinates, then contacted me. They tracked you to about a hundred miles out in stealth, then you suddenly started showing up on Air Traffic Control radar, and we saw a meteor go overhead. What the hell happened?"

"Inertial compensator failure on re-entry."

Re-entry? Skip blinked. This was no stealth jet; it was some sort of spaceship!

"I was able to keep it together coming down from the Helix Drive test range and then during re-entry over the coast, then I started to lose roll stabilization. I had to hit the Drive to steady it down and slew it in an 'S' curve to dump altitude, but you know how the Drive behaves in atmo. I barely pulled it out in time to hit the gravitic dampeners and set her down before we slammed into that hillside. She's pretty banged up. The front landing leg's gone, and my own leg took a pretty good knock."

Helix Drive? Gravitic dampener? This...even for the twenty-first century, this was something out of science fiction!

"Actually, a remnant of the front strut is doing a passing imitation of a meteor for the local sheriff's department. I found it last night. Word from on high is that we don't want local law in on this, so I gave him something to divert him. We pulled a nice chunk of it out of a furrow down in the valley. All that delta-vee you dumped went into that one piece, and it will soon have pride of place as the camp's first silica-iron meteorite."

"Camp? Then we're not blown?"

"Yes, you—we—were very lucky. You're on private property, the LEOs bought the meteor story, and the natives are friendly."

"And this is one of them?" Mike gestured at Skip.

"None other than America's patriotic, milk-drinking finest. We're in the Eagle Ridge Boy Scout Campgrounds, chock full of Eagle Scouts like this fine young fellow here. You couldn't have chosen a better spot for an impromptu set down."

Skip couldn't stand it any longer. "Sir? If you don't mind my asking, since I'm sworn to silence, what is this?"

Donnie looked at Mike and laughed. "Well, since he's seen it, and he's more than capable of putting two and two together, it's hardly a secret at this point. I'll let Mike tell you, it's his baby."

"Well, Mr. Davis, this is Delta Sierra Sierra Charlie Foxtrot Xray five niner, as you heard him say. 'DSSC' is Deep Space Survey Command, 'F' means flight, and this is the prototype of the 'Xray five niner' which means the X59 Survey Spaceplane, a one or two-person ground-to-orbit-to-deep space exploration vehicle. It's nominally based on a near-space fighter, but this model has been designated for black-space operations with a new drive that cuts transit time. I was returning from a drive test out past Lunar Farside when I had the power failure. I was supposed to land at Oak Ridge, not Eagle Ridge. Which is where, exactly?"

Skip had more questions, but given Donnie's caution earlier, he decided to wait.

"North Carolina, Mike, the northwestern corner."

"Ah, all right. Well, at least I'm not too far off course. Donnie, we've got a load of problems. We can't fly it out of here, we can't lift it off this hillside, and we damn sure can't leave it. This prototype doesn't have a passive self-destruct, and if we blow it, it will make a big bang that may draw undesirable attention. Not to mention the fact that I've now gone twenty-six hours without food or water, and there is definitely something wrong with my ankle."

"Major Lukasz, if you'll let me, perhaps I can do something for you."

The pilot stared at him skeptically. "You got the merit badge, I suppose?"

Donnie laughed. "The kid is in med school, Mike, so let him have a look. Or, you know, keep sitting there on your ass with a busted ankle, whatever suits you better."

Skip had left the first-responder bag and field auto-doc in the Jeep, but he had his compact first aid kit in his backpack, having left the larger first responder bag back in the Jeep. Donnie, meanwhile, handed Mike a bottle of water and a sandwich. Skip crouched down to look at the ankle and concluded it would probably be necessary to cut off the boot to properly get at the man's foot. "I think we should leave your boot in place. I can splint and brace it for now, then run the autodoc on it later," he told Mike, unfolding the compact splint from the kit.

Mike nodded absently. He was too busy eating to care. Between mouthfuls, he managed to address Donnie. "If this place is as secluded as you say, we could use the *Heavy Lifter* to extricate the bird, but we'd still have to do it at night."

"Small problem, Mike. It's at Downey."

"It wouldn't take that long to get it here from California."

"She's only tied up for another week, but it could take two more weeks to get her here since she can only fly at night."

"Excuse me, sir, but what's a heavy lifter?" Skip finished the splint and helped Mike up so he could sit on a fallen tree trunk instead of the dewy ground. "I'm sure Keith can call in some favors. He seems to know everybody. Our Senator camped here as a boy. We could probably borrow some heavy equipment from Liberty-Johnson, or Cherry Point."

"I'm sure we could, Skip," Donnie said, "but not without exposure to the base commanders and the officers in charge of the equipment depots. We're not just trying to keep it from the public's eyes, we can't let the local military or law enforcement know about it either. The *Heavy Lifter* is an airship with a low radar profile. It's virtually silent, and it's lift capability is augmented with reactionless thrusters. It can lift the X59 out of here quietly and transfer it to Oak Ridge by night, but we have to get it here first. Right now, it's in L.A. at the Olympics, masquerading as a blimp."

"You're kidding!" Skip said, incredulous.

"Well, you know, 'hide in plain sight' and all that. We'll sort that out later. Right now, we need to get Major Lukasz fed and watered, and then let you take proper care of his ankle."

"Do you think we can move him down to the log cabin? It's set up as an emergency shelter for backpackers during the off season. There's no one due out here for the rest of the week, and I've the field autodoc in my Jeep, so we can patch him up right."

"Mike, can you set up some sensors to watch the X, or does someone have to stay here?"

"How far away is this cabin? I'm not in any shape to guard her, and Skip here doesn't have any clearances, so unless you want to volunteer, I say we trust your meteorite dodge."

Skip pretended not to notice that the injured man didn't answer the question directly as Donnie replied. "It's about a quarter mile. Mostly downhill. We left Skip's Jeep there and hiked up. We could probably carry you the distance in about ten to fifteen minutes if we clear out a trail."

Mike thought about it a moment. Then he shook his head. "Mr. Davis seems to have done a good job here. If I can borrow that hiking stick and maybe lean on one of you, I can make it. I don't think we want to make an obvious trail."

Before they departed for the cabin, Mike instructed Donnie to remove a tablet-like device and two clear, thumb-sized chips out of the cockpit, and to place a pair of half-inch black cubes up in trees near the edge of the site. After that, Donnie and Skip assisted the pilot down the mountainside to the cabin. They had barely walked through the door when Mike fired up his tablet to check the views from the sensors left behind at the crash site.

"How long will they last?" Skip asked.

"Longer than we dare leave that bird up on the mountain," Donnie replied grimly.

Once they'd gotten the major comfortable, Skip removed the temporary splint. He barely managed to get the boot off without cutting it apart, but it was obvious that Mike wouldn't be putting it back on again anytime soon. The ankle wasn't broken, fortunately, just badly sprained. He ran the autodoc over it, and the instrument injected some regen stimulants and pain relievers into the tissue. He then put an air splint on it to help stabilize the joint while the medicine worked. Meanwhile, Donnie called Keith to report in. After getting off the phone, Donnie announced that Skip was to meet with the campmaster, who would arrange for Donnie's relief so Donnie could rejoin his nephew at dinner call.

But before he drove back to the camp offices, Skip asked Donnie to step outside; a question had been bothering him. "Sir? I thought you said you flew for an airline."

Donnie smiled. "No, I just let you believe I did. What I said was that I was a pilot and instructor, and that's exactly what I am. I ride along on check flights and write reports on deconfliction...that's basically when an atmospheric or suborbital transport encounters something that shouldn't be there. I have an office full of people who think up ways to handle those incidents. It carries the rank of captain so I can command a flight crew if need be. That's my day job, but I do it as a contractor for several airlines and one of the suborbital spacelines, as well, but not as an employee. It gives me cover to move freely around the country for my *other* job. I'm a reservist in the Space Command, seconded to a special project. I'm on active duty about as much as your typical reservist, but I spend a lot more *unofficial* time on it. Mike and I are both O-5—majors—in Space Command.

"Where are you based, Area 51?"

Donnie laughed. "We do have a group at Groom Lake, but actually our HQ is outside Los Angeles."

"But if this is just standard space technology, why the secrecy?"

"Well..." Donnie paused, and it was clear he was carefully choosing his next words. "There's a lot more at stake, here. There's developments that well...we need to keep those close to the vest."

"Like, what was it Mike said...the Helix Drive?"

Donnie turned and looked sternly at Skip. When next he spoke, his voice was like ice. "Son, you need to forget you ever heard that. Mike was in pain. He didn't know what he was saying."

"Oh. Okay. Sorry, sir. Forgotten."

"Good. It needs to stay that way. Maybe..." Donnie broke off. "Well, we'll see." After another pause, his voice and expression softened. "Anyway, there's always a chance this was not an accident, and we need to keep it quiet."

"Oh...I understand." Skip deliberately decided not to pursue the earlier line of thought any further. "How long do you think you'll be able to keep it quiet?"

Donnie—Major Donelly, Skip reminded himself—looked thoughtful. "Years, if we're lucky. But that will all depend upon what happens in the next few days."

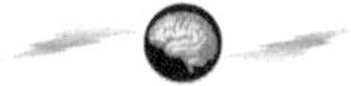

Upon his return, Skip learned that the National Guard and the sheriff's men had finally left the camp after overseeing the spraying down of last night's 'meteor' landing. However, no sooner had he gotten there than he was sent back to the cabin via the more direct route to bring Donnie his secure satellite phone. Keith had asked the camp's ranger to accompany them back to the cabin, but there had been a report of a racoon acting strangely near one of the camps, and Ranger Stephens was needed in case the animal appeared rabid. Instead, Stephen's wife, Kesha, a retired nurse, would accompany Keith and Skip back to the cabin. Kesha would stay at the cabin for the day in Donnie's place to help keep an eye on Lukasz as well as his grounded bird.

Both Skip and Donnie had to get back into normal camp routine to avoid questions. After all, their absence was noted at breakfast, and about the worst way to keep the X59 secret, short of uploading a video of it to the net, would be to inspire several dozen curious young Scouts to start asking questions about their whereabouts.

Getting back to the cabin this time was a lot easier and faster than the route through Beaver Creek. The cabin had been built as a history and conservation project and now served as an emergency overnight shelter for small group hiking and climbing. It was meant to be easy to access; the purpose of convoluted route they took earlier was to avoiding the sheriff.

Keith had brought a cooler full of food for Kesha and the major as well as a small camp stove. Upon arrival, the first thing he did was make coffee for the grateful major while Kesha fussed over Skip's first-aid ministrations from earlier. The five of them crowded around the cabin's small table.

Donnie had bad news. "I called Downey. They can't get the lifter here before mid-July. But you can't hide in this cabin for two and a half weeks, Mike. People will notice. And we can't just leave the bird sitting exposed on the mountain that long! Someone is bound to stumble across it or pick it up on satellite. Is there any way we could carry it off somehow? If we could get it on a truck, we could move it somewhere secure under cover."

"If I can realign the platform, I can get the inertial compensators online for as long as the battery lasts. It won't last long, maybe an hour. That would negate most of its weight. Six or eight people could theoretically lift it, but it would be pretty unwieldy, even on a flat surface. Once the battery runs out, it will be too heavy for a truck to safely carry. An hour would barely be enough time to get it off the mountainside, assuming we could even manage it."

"What kind of power do you need?" asked Kesha. "Steve's got plenty of tools and supplies at the maintenance shed. He's got spare batteries for the solar array, would they do? We could even rig up some panels as a generator."

"It's got to be compact and light. The compensators won't offset the battery's weight, and we'll need about 50 volts at high drain. A fuel cell would be better. I'm going to need a collimating beam for the stabilizers; a *good* laser pointer will probably work. And then we need to figure out where we're going to store it that's secure and out of sight, but close enough to keep watch."

"Why not hide it in plain sight?" Skip asked. "It works for the *Lifter*, right?"

Major Lukasz looked doubtful. "What do you mean by that? We can't exactly park it at the local airport and try to pass it off as a Cessna!"

"We could paint *Epic Games* on the side and tell everyone it's their corporate jet," Donnie said wryly. Only Skip laughed; the other three just looked at him blankly. That made Donnie laugh. "Never mind. What are you thinking, Kay-det?"

"Look, Mr. Keith, you're always saying you want to get more campers interested in the camp museum. I remember an astronaut turned actor Uncle Bill told me about. He was at camp something like twenty years ago. I heard he just made a movie last year, a science fiction one. Can't we pretend this is a prop from one of his movies? Better yet, dress it up as retro-sci-fi, like some of the twentieth-century stuff? If we put science fiction space stuff around it, I doubt it would stand out at all."

"Pretty thin story, especially if anyone has seen that guy's movies." Mike obviously was not a fan.

"We don't need to pass it off as anything. We're not actually going to show it to anyone, we just need to have a good excuse to cart something that size onto the grounds and leave it sitting there for a few weeks."

"Oh," Mike said, rubbing his chin. "Now that's different."

Keith nodded slowly. "Let's think about this. We'd want to do it on Saturday, after this week's campers leave, so there won't be anyone around except staffers. They won't notice if a few people are missing for an evening because there is always turnover on the weekends. So, if we can get it off the mountain, we just move it down into camp, put it someplace central, lock it up tight, and tell everyone it's a prop on loan from Rick Bustamante for the museum."

"How are we going to explain it when it vanishes overnight in three weeks?"

"We don't." Keith grinned at Kesha. "There's a prop shop down in the 'Lottie district of Char-Salem. Hang some fiberboard on the real thing, then send sketches to the shop and have them build us a prop out of fiber. Stash the prop in Steve and Kesha's workshop and swap it for your ship on moving day."

The two majors looked at each other. "That could actually work," Donnie said.

Mike nodded. "It's probably less risky than renting out a warehouse and leaving a paper trail."

"I asked Rick about getting some items last year, and he said to call his studio if I wanted anything. This is probably a bigger favor than he was expecting, but we can say we're promoting the museum. If I recall right, they had at least four different designs of space fighters; one might even suit our needs as is. If we park it on the old parade ground in front of the classroom building and build a "box" around it with just enough gaps to tease folks with a glimpse inside, no one will know what is *really* in it."

"Doesn't sound very secure, though," Mike objected. "Even if it is covered up, leaving it right out in the open like that?"

"Mike, the camp's health lodge is right across from the parade ground. You can stay in the bunkroom in the back. S.C. has daily shifts there already, and Kesha's on call. You'll not only have eyes on your plane, you'll be within 50 feet of it at all times. And if S.C. doesn't mind having his quarters upgraded for the next few weeks, we'll move him in there with you."

Skip didn't mind at all. There were a lot of other details still to work out, but by the time Keith decided it was time to get back, everyone admitted that his idea was a workable one. The lodge would make a comfortable operations center for Mike, it was central to everything in camp, and the X59 would fit easily on the parade ground.

"Folks, I think we have a plan," Donnie said. "I'll check on batteries or fuel cells. Davis, may I borrow that laser pointer you use for your astronomy classes?"

"Yes, sir. I'll have to retrieve it from my quarters."

"Good, that may suffice. We'll try it out just to be sure."

"One more thing," Donnie said. "We can't be calling it the spaceship or the X-59. We need a code word for the project. Skip, you spotted her first, so why don't you do the honors."

Skip thought for a moment. "How about NIGHTFALL?"

"That sounds vague enough," Mike said.

"Works for me," Donnie agreed, and winked at Skip. "We'll just hope the natives don't get scared and burn down the camp, right, Kay-det? NIGHTFALL it is."

At that point, Keith decided they had better leave if they were to make the dining assembly at eighteen hundred. Skip drove him and Donnie back to the central camp and off to their individual quarters to shower and change their clothes. Skip wondered if he actually had any clean clothes or if he'd need to make a trip to the laundry. He grinned. Camp life was going to seem a little mundane after the last twenty-four hours, but with the camp full of teens, his counselor duties weren't the sort of thing that could be put on hold for long, not even for mysterious spaceships falling out of the night sky.

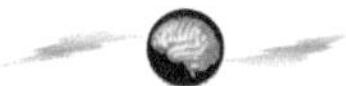

The next day, Donnie drove into town early. He returned an hour later, borrowed the laser pointer from Skip, then disappeared for the rest of the day. Skip had to stay in camp and administer the final astronomy test, then attend a staff meeting after lunch. Keith waited for the program director to finish announcements after which he addressed the staff.

"Gentlemen and ladies." There were giggles from the younger staff and stern looks from the older ones. "We are announcing a new theme for the rest of the summer. I know some of you are scheduled to rotate out or will be joining your families for vacation, but I encourage those of you who will be here to consider this new theme in your courses.

"We know the kids and their families come here out of nostalgia or adventure. Kids from domes or conurbs may have never been under an open sky, so we normally stress the outdoors, camping, and historical recreation. However, the star of last year's TriVee *Asteroid Pirates* was a former camper and has donated a new display for the camp museum! He's offered to loan us props from his movie, and we're going to offer some "retro space exploration" from the perspective of our twentieth century campers who experienced the first moon landing and space stations. We're even going to include some of the nineteenth century concepts by Verne and Meliere, since they tend to be 'ret-chill' as you young folk say."

The room came to life with everyone talking at once. You had to be at least a little bit interested in history to spend all summer away from most of the trappings of the twenty-first century. Skip knew that several area directors were well-versed in the early history of space exploration. This would be fun!

Skip was on duty at the health lodge that evening. So as not to further disrupt the work schedule, Keith visited him there. Donnie was back with his nephew's unit and would be leaving with them in the morning. Two men from Downey would be arriving just after dawn, and Skip was to meet them at the local maglev. They were taking a train up from the suborbital transit field at 'Lottie and would need local transport. Unfortunately, that could not be arranged until later in the day.

"Mike says that 'LecStor battery from the solar array and your laser will work. The plan is to move NIGHTFALL on Saturday after dark. By that time, most of the staff will be gone on 'Kiss and Klean.' I hope you don't mind, but we'll need your arms and back."

Skip nodded. That meant no leave this weekend, but he'd already assumed he'd be needed for NIGHTFALL. He didn't mind as much as he might have. His parents were in Scotland for a year for his father's work, and his girlfriend, Sara, was on summer Reserve duty as part of her scholarship. He'd been planning on going to his aunt and uncle's house this weekend, and he made a mental note to give his aunt a call and cancel so that she didn't worry.

Saturday morning, Skip drove to the small town on the edge of the Blue Ridge Protected Zone. 'Mr. Smith' and 'Mr. Jones' arrived on time on a maglev out of 'Lottie. He held up his tablet, with the screen reading 'Eagle Ridge Camp' in large letters, and wondered if he should have put any other identifying information on it. 'Survey Command' or 'X-59' would have guaranteed their attention, but he assumed that would be a security breach which would not go over well. A man and a woman in dark suits and dark glasses stopped about ten feet away and looked as if they might be Smith and Jones; after all, no one had mentioned whether they were male or female. Just when Skip was about to approach them, two men in bright polo shirts and khaki slacks walked up and introduced themselves. They each had large duffel bags, and Jones carried what looked like a tool box. They tossed their gear in the back of the jeep and continued a cheerful conversation throughout the thirty-minute drive back to camp. As they left the station, Davis noticed the dark-suited couple getting into a black car that didn't appear to be a rental. Skip shrugged and promptly dismissed them.

Once at camp, things got hectic. Kesha brought Mike Lukasz down to the health lodge to recheck his ankle. Keith was waiting there to take the two newcomers to the crash site. As Kesha did her examination, Skip took the opportunity to look at Mike's ankle; the autodoc had dealt with the swelling, and the regen meds had improved the skin color and muscle strength. Overall, it was looking much better. With a protective skin wrap and reinforced with the major's high boots, it was more secure than if it had been immediately placed in a cast. The four older men returned to the crash site, so Skip went back to quarters to do his laundry and pack up for his temporary move to the lodge.

To his surprise, he discovered that with Keith and the camp ranger out at the crash site, he was now the senior member out of the dozen or so staffers left in camp. That meant doubling as medic and Officer of the Day, which also meant taking phone calls and meeting visitors. He was expecting the scheduled dining hall food delivery, so he wasn't surprised to get called out to the gate, but he was surprised to find a private freight service truck waiting there. The driver had a rush order for the 'Space Camp Scouts' from a film studio in Great'Lanta. Skip directed them to unload the crates at the camp museum; and the driver and assistant quickly unloaded the crates without help, leaving Skip free to read over the manifests: *Apollo 13* space suit, *Interstellar* AI robot, *The Martian* rover mockup, *Alcubierre* control computer, *Asteroid Pirates* remote manipulator arm control station, and more. A lot more.

Wow! he thought, impressed. There were some classics here!

It was approaching seventeen hundred when Keith called Skip and told him to dress for dinner in town and leave Jenny, the next senior staffer, in charge. His laundry wasn't finished, but fortunately, he still had a clean pair of khakis and a polo shirt for the air-conditioned restaurant. When Donnie drove up, Skip was surprised to see his Uncle Bill sitting in the passenger seat. His uncle proceeded to tell him how he had been awakened at six AM by a phone call from Skip's father, who had in turn been awakened at one AM Glasgow time by an old friend calling from the office of the Secretary of Defense, needing to fast-track security clearance for one S.C. Davis.

"Well, Skip, you've caused quite a stir. Your dad wanted to know why you needed a security clearance, and why it had landed on Russell's desk. Your mother convinced him to at least wait until I had a reasonable chance of waking up enough to find out. Then Don here showed up knocking at my door at noon and filled me in. I called Keith, and he suggested Donnie and I come up and discuss a few things with you and the others over dinner. My recommendation is that you order yourself a steak, we're going to want everyone at full strength before we tackle NIGHTFALL."

"Wait a minute. How does Dad know anyone at the office of the Secretary of Defense?"

"It turns out you're not the only one able to keep a secret, Kay-det. Your father has been working with the DoD for a long time," said Donnie.

"What? Dad works for them?"

Skip's eyes only got wider as his uncle laughed and said: "*With them,* Skip, not for them. For that matter, so do I, occasionally. Look, Skip. I know you turned down the ROTC scholarship and took the civilian one instead, but you may want to rethink your career path."

Skip frowned and shook his head. "You know I don't want to get involved with the military right now, Uncle Bill. Sara's going to have a service commitment for at least eight years after she graduates, and we can't exactly get married if we're stationed on different continents, or even different planets!"

"Don't worry, Kay-det. You're not being drafted, and you wouldn't be put on active duty in any case. We had something like a Reserve commission in mind. As long as the security check on you and your fiancé is clean, and I can't imagine it wouldn't be for a literal Boy Scout like you, we'll find a place for both of you in DSS."

Skip didn't know what to think. A Reserve commission as an officer in a secret Space Force project? To say nothing of what suddenly seemed like his entire family working on the sly with the military? He didn't drink alcohol, but for the first time in his life, he felt like he understood the concept of needing a drink.

They joined the others for an uneventful dinner except for one curious event. The appetizers had just been cleared away when Skip caught a glimpse of a couple at a table away from the entrance. It was, he thought, the dark-suited couple from the airport, although he was wearing a dark blue pullover and jeans and she was in a light blue dress. They didn't appear to be close enough to overhear their conversation and seemed to be in a conversation of their own, but Skip thought it too great a coincidence.

You're just being paranoid, he told himself. But was he? They were hiding a top-secret spacecraft, so how could he know what was really of concern and what was not?

When Donnie excused himself to head to the restroom, Skip waited a minute, then did the same, catching Donnie while he was washing his hands. When he mentioned the couple from the airport being at the restaurant, Donnie reassured him. "Good eye, Kay-det. Jones spotted them this morning. Don't worry, I made a call. We let some people know they'd been spotted. They won't be a problem."

Not entirely reassured, Skip followed Donnie back to the table. Before long, the couple finished their meal, paid, and left, so Skip tried to put them out of his mind. It wasn't hard to do once the waitress delivered his ribeye steak—real steak, not vat-grown protein. The conversation died down as he and the others turned their attention to the food, which was considerably better than what the camp cooks were able to serve despite their best efforts. All too soon, the dinner was over. Keith had decided they would return to camp by twenty hundred, change, and head out for the crash site.

The goal was to move NIGHTFALL at midnight. Donnie had been in touch with DSS, and they had assured him there would be no "eyes in the sky" watching at that time. They were all gathered around the downed X-59 more than fifteen minutes early. The actual move turned out to be much less eventful than Skip had feared. Mike had recalibrated his gyros and rigged up a power cable to the battery pack. The pilot was fairly confident he could get more than an hour out of the inertial compensators, and they had a larger battery waiting on the truck. Still, Mike needed to stay in the cockpit to monitor power levels and balance the weight compensation. There were seven of them there, but with Mike in the cockpit, that left Skip, Keith, Uncle Bill, Donnie, Smith, and Jones to do the heavy lifting.

A low, nearly inaudible hum signaled that Mike had turned on the ship's systems. The six men stationed themselves around the ship and lifted, which allowed Mike to use a little of the precious battery power to raise the two remaining landing legs to give them easier clearance. With the inertial compensators doing most of the work, they half-carried, half-guided the X59 down the two hundred yards that separated the crash site from a flatbed trailer hitched to one of the camp's utility vehicles.

Thanks to the compensators, NIGHTFALL didn't feel much heavier to Skip than carrying furniture up and down the stairs in his college apartment. But the ground was uneven, the footing was slippery, and even with bright lights shining up from the trailer, it was nearly impossible for him to look down and see where he was stepping. They proceeded slowly, straining, and grunting, listening as Donnie or Jones pointed out a root, a fallen branch, or a rock in the way, then feeling the way along with their feet. And, of course, there was always the minor concern that if the inertial compensators were to unexpectedly fail or run out of juice sooner than expected, everyone except Mike and Uncle Bill would be badly injured.

Eventually, they came within sight of the tractor, and step-by-step, they brought NIGHTFALL closer to the flatbed. It had been decided that a wheeled vehicle was necessary, and not a ground effect floater, so the last ten yards went agonizingly slowly as they manually positioned the X-59 over the trailer instead of sliding the trailer under the ship. Mike ordered them to step back as he boosted the compensators momentarily; then decreased them again once everyone was clear. The trailer bed visibly sagged as it took more of NIGHTFALL's true weight.

Keith had picked a good weekend for the move. The Fourth of July fell in the middle of the next week, so there were no temporary counselors-in-training scheduled for the weekend or following week. Before they'd left the camp's grounds, he had counted the cars in the parking lot and personally confirmed where every staff member on the premises was located. Most of them were watching TriVee in the dining hall.

He drove ahead with Skip and went from building to building, bunk to bunk, to ensure that everyone was still accounted for as the trailer arrived in front of the program center two hours later. This was going to be the tricky part. They couldn't risk physically lifting the craft off the trailer in case the power failed and dropped NIGHTFALL's full weight on their shoulders. But Mike had switched over to the secondary battery bank on the trailer. The cabling wouldn't stretch very far, and would only provide about five minutes of power, but it should suffice for the next maneuver.

They stood well clear and watched with anticipation as Mike powered the compensators well past the previous level, then lifted NIGHTFALL up from the overloaded trailer. It floated with deceptive ease over to a stone and cinderblock stand as Donnie, with one hand on the craft's nose, guided it into position. He held up his hand and gave Mike a thumb's up, at which point Mike powered down the system. Skip watched with the others as the blocks sunk deeply into the ground as the inertial compensation shut down. There was no shifting or settling; Donnie and Keith had arranged it well.

And then the hard work began. First, they had to drag out the long plastiwood beams and construct a frame around NIGHTFALL. It took less than thirty minutes to completely encase NIGHTFALL in a five-sided plastiwood box, but to Skip's aching back, it felt more like thirty hours. Stephens assured the four government folks that he would drill bolts into the cinderblocks first thing in the morning, thereby ensuring it would be nearly impossible for anyone to clearly see what was inside the wooden frame.

Smith and Jones were flying back at noon tomorrow from the big 'port in 'Lottie. Donnie took charge of getting them back to the mag-lev, leaving Keith to drive Uncle Bill back to Salem. Before everyone split up in search of their beds, though, Mike Lukasz showed them the two palm-sized components Skip had seen him pull out of NIGHTFALL's cockpit the other day. "Got someplace we can lock these up?" he asked.

"Certainly," said Keith. "There's a safe in the admin building and a drug lockup in the lodge where you're staying if you want to keep them close."

"Good. I like having them nearby, but let's split them up. They've got flight data on them, in addition to other things, so we'll need them to figure out what went wrong with the bird."

That settled, they split up, and Skip retired to his new quarters at the nearby health lodge with Mike to keep him company. He let Mike take the room with the window overlooking his boxed-up vehicle and threw himself down on the bed in the other room without even undressing. No sooner had his head hit the pillow than he was sound asleep.

Skip realized that with all the activity of the past few days, he'd been missed by his friends on staff. He'd had to make excuses for not joining his friends Chad Jacobs and Claire Liu, both counselors but in other areas, for dinner in town on Saturday. It was supposed to have been pizza and beer, the former rare and the latter forbidden in camp. They were disappointed and more than a bit curious, so he blamed it on taking over the health officer job.

The next day, Sunday, was the day new campers arrived, and the camp was bustling from the moment the sun rose as staff members returned and prepared the campsites and program areas. There was no reveille, morning assembly or mess hall breakfast service on Sunday, so Skip slept in. There was a staff meeting at eleven, though, and he could see vehicles starting to line up to drop off the week's campers. There would be no driving in camp today, it was simply too busy, but Skip was surprised to learn that he would be one of the exceptions. He had been authorized to drive one of the "golf carts"—two-seat solar-electric runabouts—so he could ferry Mike Lukasz and his healing ankle around camp. The pilot's cover was that he was a representative from the Kansas Cosmodrome, working with the camp museum. An unfortunate accident with a dropped crate had injured his foot, and it was decided that he should stay and rest while assisting with the new display.

Skip's cover, meant to explain why he'd moved quarters, was that he was taking over as the camp's official health officer. The former HO had to head home early to the Pensaco-Mobile. A storm had developed too quickly for Weather Control and his hospital was overloaded. Fortunately, for his peace of mind, Eagle Ridge always supplemented the health lodge staff with physicians who attended camp with their kids, and this week there were two: an internal medicine professor from in-state and an emergency medicine doc from 'Lottie. Skip was glad they no longer had to perform health checks as the campers arrived. Each person's was issued a medi-quik chip pre-camp, and it was electronically registered on arrival. It was a good thing, too. Between the late-night moving NIGHTFALL and moving quarters, Skip was still operating on a sleep deficit. To his surprise, Mike turned out to be a significant asset. The two of them inventoried the stock of bee sting and poison ivy medicines, and Mike replenished the supply of bottled water and electrolytes with a quick cart run to the dining hall. Those supplies might be important because the forecast called for a hot week; Keith had already announced that it was too hot for formal parade ground activities before dinner and that all of the welcoming ceremonies would be held as part of the evening program.

Even with the crowd of new campers, parents, and returning camp staff, Skip tried to keep a watch out for any unusual activity as he'd been told. Hiding in plain sight seemed to be working, but that was no reason to let down their guard. Skip, himself, had had at least ten conversations with staffers and incoming campers about the mysterious crate in front of the museum.

Like many buildings in camp, the Health Lodge was a throwback to the early twentieth century—styled like an old farmhouse with a porch on two sides. It was central to the camp, so he could see the line of incoming campers as they were scanned into the database over at the admin building. Skip watched the new arrivals as they went through the process, and two individuals stood out to him in particular. One was a tall, imposing man with what appeared to be Pacific Islander heritage. He was at least six-and-a-half feet in height, heavily muscled, and wore a tight-fitting black shirt and black cargo pants despite the heat. He wore sunglasses, so it wasn't possible to see his eyes, but Skip had the impression that he was carefully taking in the surrounding area. The second man was as different from the first as could be. He was pale skinned—possibly Northern European—short, rotund, visibly sweating, and extremely red in the face from the heat. He wore a loose, white guayabera shirt over khaki shorts, and round wire-rimmed glasses covered bulging eyes that were in constant motion. He was wearing a white straw hat and constantly mopped his face with a soaked red bandana. The one thing he had in common with the other noticeable new arrival was that he, too, seemed inordinately interested in the camp's grounds.

His suspicions aroused, he wandered over to talk with Chad and Claire who were monitoring the younger staff conducting the check-in. The records showed the big guy was Jeremy Otago, with one of the Char-Salem troops in camp this week. The red-faced man was Richard Lewis, from a troop based out west. When Skip shared his concerns with Mike, he discovered that Mike had also had some concerns about the two men. For example, while Otago was with a unit based in an urban center, he wore well-worn hiking boots, a rescue-style belt made from wrapped parachute cord, and he seemed oblivious to the heat and insects. Lewis, meanwhile, was supposedly from an agridistrict, yet he wore expensive synthetic clothes and a designer watch—not to mention that he didn't seem to be tolerating the heat and humidity very well. After comparing notes, they agreed that both men bore watching throughout the week.

Despite the changes in his responsibilities, Skip still had to work the mess hall serving line once a day, and today he was on dinner duty. Mike volunteered to take a turn; the better to fit in with the rest of the staff. So, Skip served out the hot plates while Mike sat on a tall stool and handed prepackaged beverages and rolls to the campers as they walked through the line. The silver lining was the chance to look over all the campers again, including Otago and Lewis.

At the campfire program that evening, Keith announced the museum additions and movie props to the campers to considerable applause. Campers were warned that some of the items were fragile constructions and not to be touched. No mention was made of the large crate resting on the side of the parade ground. Thursday was the Fourth of July, but a special Wednesday night campfire was planned with fireworks and special events to which the parents were invited for a special Family Night.

The next few days went by quickly as the camp gradually turned into a space-themed adventure, mostly without incident. There were the usual scrapes and sprains to address in the health lodge, but the two physicians were often around to help. Mike took over the astronomy classes, for which he was eminently suited, so Skip's duties, beyond keeping an eye on NIGHTFALL, mainly consisted of caring for the inevitable cases of heatstroke, rashes, sprains, cuts, and stings. Infusions of water, electrolytes, and an hour or so of rest inside the cool, dry lodge were usually enough. Despite the heat, they made it to Wednesday with only one boy needing to go to the county hospital.

Keith came by in the afternoon to talk to them. "It's Family Night, so we're going to have a lot of strangers in camp tonight. If anyone is going to try to sneak in, tonight would be the night. You two should probably stick close to NIGHTFALL and skip the evening campfire."

Skip didn't mind, but once again, he'd have to come up with an excuse to tell Chad and Claire. When they weren't involved in skits or songs, they usually sat together. At least he and Mike would still be able to see the fireworks over The Knob from the porch.

They set up chairs where they could keep an eye on the parade ground, hear the music from the amphitheater and still see the fireworks. Mike produced a six-pack of contraband cold beer from a cooler and offered one to Skip, who declined with a smile. The pilot shrugged, cracked open a can, and raised it in an ironic salute. It was about twenty-one thirty and mostly dark; the gathering at the campfire was well underway when Mike nudged Skip and pointed to a shadow moving near the giant wooden crate. Skip had a light—not as powerful as the one they'd used last week, but still pretty bright—and pointed it in that direction, but neither of them could see anyone near NIGHTFALL.

At Mike's urging, Skip left the porch and quickly walked over to check the area. He saw a few footprints, and it looked as if someone might have been trying to pry at the boards, but there was no one there. Mike grabbed the big light and methodically shone it around the areas with the deepest shadows, but it exposed nothing but a wide-eyed fox. After that, Skip gave up, returned to the porch, and they waited for the fireworks. The show was a good one, but near the end, during the grand finale, he thought he saw a flash or two near ground level. It might have been a camera flash, or it could have just been a reflection off a window.

Was someone taking a picture of the plastiwood crate? What would that prove? The thought chilled him. What if someone was sneaking around and needed to eliminate witnesses? He dismissed it as a silly thought and didn't say anything to Mike about it. He felt in his pocket to confirm that his utility knife was there, and that made him feel a little more prepared. He looked over at Mike and realized that the way his shirt didn't fall correctly over his lower back meant he was probably even better armed.

After breakfast the next morning, Skip wandered down to the shelter that served as a classroom for the outdoors and wilderness programs. Campers were given an hour after breakfast to clean their campsites before starting the various classes; the staff used this time to prepare for teaching them. Skip was looking for his friend Chad Jacobs, who would be there early to prepare for a day in the outback. Two years older than Skip, Chad was the lead wilderness counselor. It was an unusual job assignment considering that Chad was born and lived most of his life in the RDU conurb a hundred miles east. He was local, now; his parents had retired and bought a place about five miles from the camp's entrance. They had become rather well known among the staff and often provided an emergency home-away-from-home with laundry, transportation, and meals for those counselors who needed them.

Chad had been a hell-raiser as a boy, but his father had introduced him to metalworking, and it had changed his life. That got him into re-enactments and outdoor skills. Now, he and his father ran a blacksmith shop where he made expensive replica swords for tourists, and he ran the wilderness events for the camp. Skip needed someone with good ideas for tricks and traps, just in case a stranger really was skulking about the camp. If anyone would have ideas, it would be Chad.

Chad was doing something complicated with ropes, and he greeted Skip with little more than a raised eyebrow. "Hey, Space Cadet. How are you liking the lodge? Got to be nice sleeping in air-conditioned comfort in a nice soft bed while we're sweating in sleeping bags on the hard ground!"

"You're the doggone wilderness counselor, Chad, not the five-star hotel counselor, in case you've forgotten." Skip grinned. "And the air-conditioning is very nice on these sweltering summer nights. You know, I was actually a little chilly last night!"

He laughed as Chad groaned in not-entirely-fake envy. "Look, I have a project for you," he told the older counselor, then outlined his suspicions that someone was sneaking around the big crate on the parade ground. "We have to give that back after the big event at the end of the summer, and Mr. Keith doesn't want it damaged. They might want to use it in another movie, and I don't think the studio would appreciate people breaking off a piece of it or whatever."

"So, what's in it?"

"I could tell you, but Mr. Keith would kill both of us."

"Yeah," Chad grunted and looked thoughtful. He continued lacing his hiking boots, then pulled out a bandanna and tied it over his head. "In the conurb, I would have used lasers and inductive fields. In the wilderness, we'd probably do it with tin cans, wire, and broken glass. Mr. Keith probably wouldn't like that, so I'm thinking soft ground, a snare or two, and of course, a movement sensor."

"We can't booby trap the whole area because that would be too obvious. I'm worried about the woods between the parade ground and the creek, someone could sneak in from there. Everywhere else, we have covered from the lodge." He didn't mention that whoever had already pried at the plastiwood covering NIGHTFALL appeared to have come from the direction of the woods.

"No, that's good. It's opposite the walkway, and no one goes over there on purpose. I've got plenty of natural and artificial materials for snares. My afternoon class can learn how to make traps." He paused a moment, then continued, "So, who are you looking to catch? Any ideas?"

"There are a couple of guys here who don't seem right. A Mr. Otago with Troop 150 and a Mr. Lewis with Troop 36."

"Otago and Lewis?"

"Otago is a big dude, dark, all muscles, has some kind of allergy to colored laundry. The other guy is short, fat, wears a funny hat—I think it's called a 'Panama hat.' He has a face like a tomato."

"Darker than me?" Chad grinned, all white teeth against midnight-black skin. "Oh yeah, I know who you mean. Man Mountain and Sweathog!" It was always hard for the staffers to remember all the names of the people coming and going over the summer, so it was common to assign them nicknames. And the names were not always flattering.

"I heard from Claire that when she came back from dinner and dropped by admin that Man Mountain was in the office ,and it looked like he had been trying to get into the computer. Dude said he wanted to print some schedules for the kids in his unit. Claire got him some flexi, programmed them with the schedules, and then shooed him out. Oh, by the way, she's mad at you for bailing on the latest Four Horsemen for Earth movie on Saturday."

"I wonder what else he might have gotten into?" Skip chose to ignore the subtle dig. After all, he had a fiancé! Claire was just a friend, like Chad. Besides, the information worried him. He hoped the man hadn't been trying to get into the safe.

Chad was staring at him. "You know something you're not telling me, Space Cadet? Are you scared of something?"

"Me? Nah," Skip shook his head. "We're at camp. What is there to be scared of?"

"You tell me. Well, anyhow, I'll get you your traps before sundown. I've got to go introduce this morning's campers to the great wilderness that is Eagle Ridge! You'd better get back to your AC before you melt."

"Thanks, Chad," Skip said, embarrassed that he had trouble looking his friend in the eye. He felt bad leaving Chad in the dark, but what could he do? He'd promised not to tell anyone, and he wasn't about to break his word now.

Annoyed with him or not, Chad showed up as promised and set the traps. No one disturbed them that night. And the rest of the week also passed without incident. Otago and Lewis both left on schedule with their troops. Mike's ankle was healed up, and it was time to incorporate some exercises and therapy. Skip had come to rather like the sarcastic older man, and even Chad took to spending some of his off-duty time on the wide porch of the lodge. Mike co-opted him as a lookout when both he and Skip were occupied; however, he did not see fit to tell Chad what was in the giant crate they were guarding.

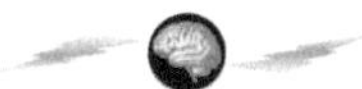

The following week fell into a pattern of morning workouts, daily classes, dining hall dinners and evening conversations with the major as they all waited for Space Command to transport the Heavy Lifter across the country. They didn't relax their vigilance, at least not purposefully, but the sense of stress and danger Skip had been feeling vanished on Saturday with Man Mountain and Sweathog.

The campers had all departed by noon, and Skip was looking forward to the peace and quiet of a Saturday evening in a newly abandoned camp. Mike was off to Oak Ridge to discuss arrangements for moving NIGHTFALL during the following week. It was the first time Mike had been away overnight since he'd come to the camp, and Skip reflected that he might have been worried if the last week hadn't been so tranquil. The crate still sat there, unmolested, and other than a young Second Class Scout caught trying to carve his patrol insignia into the plastiwood, the boards hadn't been touched since that night nearly two weeks ago.

The sun had just gone down, and there was still a line of purple-red light above the tree line on the horizon, when Skip heard the cry. It appeared to be coming from the other side of the camp, but he couldn't quite make out what the person was yelling.

"Do you hear that?" he asked Chad, who had been inside fetching a pair of sodas. The temptation to break into Mike's contraband beer was strong, but they took their jobs seriously and would save it for when they were completely away from camp.

Chad cocked his head. Then his eyes opened wide.

"I think he's saying fire!" he told Skip. They looked at each other, then Skip grabbed his phone and the Health Lodge fire extinguisher from its wall mount.

"Stay here!" he said, and he sprinted off in the direction of the alarm. The summer had been dry, and with so few people in the camp, even a small campfire could rapidly turn into a conflagration that would threaten the entire grounds!

As he ran around the corner of the dining hall, he could see a faint glow from one of the staff cabins. When he approached it, he could see two young men trying to fight the fire with dirt and a shovel, but despite their best efforts they were barely able to slow down the hungry flames.

"Why are you using dirt? Where are the fire buckets? Where's your fire extinguisher?" Skip shouted. "Did you call the fire department?"

"We can't find them!" said the counselors with the shovel. "We thought we could control it by smothering it with dirt."

"What happened?"

"I have no idea! I wasn't cooking, I wasn't ironing or anything!"

"Probably an electrical short," Skip said grimly. He handed off the fire extinguisher to the other counselor. He already had his mobile phone up to his ear. "Hello, Fire Department? We have a situation with a cabin fire at Eagle Ridge Camp..."

Keith arrived a few minutes later, by which time the cabin was thoroughly engulfed in flames. Skip, the cabin's two residents, and several other counselors were frantically clearing out brush and stamping out every stray spark that was thrown out by the fire. Upon spotting Skip and learning that the fire brigade was on their way, Keith ordered Skip back to his quarters. Sooty, sweaty, and breathing hard, Skip walked slowly back to the lodge, carrying the empty extinguisher.

As he walked back through the trees, Skip's foot connected with something metallic. He shined his flashlight on the ground. It was a fire bucket. In fact, there were two of them, lying there, empty. Camp rules required two buckets filled with water at each tent and cabin. The water had to be changed daily to keep down the mosquitos, so there was no excuse for them to be this far from a campsite. There was something wrong about that fire.

As Skip approached the lodge, the strange feeling that something was wrong...got worse. Chad wasn't out on the porch, for one thing. And for another, the interior lights were on, but in the exam rooms. He hadn't left them on, and if Mike had come back from Oak Ridge, the lights would have been on in the bunkrooms or the common area. As he got closer, he could see that the two chairs on the porch were overturned, as if there had been a struggle. Skip turned off his light, and moving as quietly as he could, he opened the door.

He could hear two voices talking. While they weren't loud enough for him to hear what they were saying, he could tell there were two male voices. One was Chad, and the other one sounded vaguely familiar, but unfriendly. He slipped through the front door as quietly as possible and carefully made his way through the short hallway past the darkened waiting rooms. The lights and voices were coming from the smaller of the two exam rooms that doubled as an office for the Health Officer; it had a desk, phone, computer...and the drug lockup! Was that what this was all about, some local meth-head looking for a score? He didn't dare call for help until he had some idea what the situation was.

"I told you, you idiot! I don't have the key or the combination! I don't know anything about the safe. I don't work here! I'm the wilderness counselor. I'm just a friend of the guy who works here!"

Skip was close enough now to catch a glimpse of the man through the partially opened door. The man's back was toward him, but he recognized him from two weeks before. It was the red-faced man, the one they'd called Sweathog. Skip thought for a moment—what was his name? Oh, yes, Lewis. Lewis was searching through desk drawers in Skip's office, probably looking to see if he had been foolish enough to write down the combination. Chad was seated in a wooden chair beside the desk, his wrists and ankles held to the chair by plastic zip ties. He wasn't going anywhere, not until Skip could free him. They'd have to be cut to get him loose. Skip pulled out his utility knife—it was a good one with a custom blade; it had been handmade for him by Chad. Still, he wished he had Donnie's machete, or better yet, his gun.

Lewis grunted and went back to rummaging through the office, found a drawer with tools, and pulled out a screwdriver. "Well, if you don't have the combination, I'll just have to pry this box off the wall."

It was at that point that Skip realized what Lewis was after. The components from NIGHTFALL! If Lewis got the box free from the wall, he didn't need to open it here. He could take it with him and open it somewhere with the appropriate tools. The box was meant to secure medicines brought to camp; it wasn't a heavy-duty safe. The lockbox was firmly anchored, but the health lodge was a restored farmhouse. The material could splinter, and enough force could get the lockbox loose.

Skip backed away from the door to see what he had that could be used to stop Lewis. Nothing much: his knife and the jeep keys in his pocket, his phone, a short length of climbing rope, and a flashlight.   There was just enough light coming through the door to see around the room.   Oh! One of the rope-and-branch traps Chad's class had built was still by the front door. Now he just needed something really heavy...and to get Lewis out of the back room. The man seemed content to stay where he was and threaten Chad. That would give him the advantage against anyone coming through the office door. Skip needed to make sure Lewis was curious enough to come out and look.

Moving as slowly and quietly as he could manage, Skip set his trap in the door to the exam room. He stretched a length of rope across the doorway and placed the trap where it was most likely to be stepped on. He entered a command and then placed his phone just out of sight at the end of the exam table. He stepped carefully over the rope and trap, then retreated to the waiting room to rest until the alarm went off.

BUZZ! The phone sounded like a horde of angry bees, but there was no way it could be confused with normal insect sounds. This was the alarm Skip used on weekdays during college and med school. He'd never missed a class, nor been late, no matter how late he'd stayed up studying the increasingly difficult medical curriculum. This was an alarm that could not be ignored.

He could hear a raised voice from the office. "What's that noise?" Skip couldn't hear Chad's reply, but Lewis must not have liked it, since the next sound was a slap. The alarm went quiet, then started again a minute later. After several minutes, and many swear words, there was the sound of footsteps, and Skip could see the shadows and silhouette as Lewis came out of the office. Fortunately, the rest of the health lodge was dark, and Lewis had not turned on any more lights. The figure moved toward the exam room.

There was a snap, a muffled cry, a thump, and a clatter. Skip moved quickly, swinging the empty fire extinguisher high to hit Lewis on the head, but it was not necessary. The man was on the ground, feet tangled in the rope and trap, hands empty and spread wide. Apparently, the clatter had been a rather large knife sliding across the floor to the other side of the room. Lewis wasn't moving, so Skip's First Aid instincts took over. He put down the fire extinguisher and moved over to check for a pulse...OK, slow pulse. He was breathing, too. Skip stood back, then reached up to turn on the room light. There was a large red welt, a slight cut, and some blood on Lewis' forehead. He seemed to have knocked himself out without the aid of Skip's makeshift club.

Skip pulled the rest of the rope from where he had attached the makeshift tripwire. A few extra loops went around the man's ankles and wrists. He then turned the heavy man onto his side so there would be no breathing problems until he woke up.

He heard the sound of someone clapping. "Gutsy move, son. What if he'd been faking?" Skip grabbed the fire extinguisher again as he turned around. The man in doorway quickly held up his empty hands. "I'm friendly, Mr. Davis."

"Man Mountain?" Skip almost choked the words back in time. "I mean, Mr. Otago?"

"Master Sergeant Otago, actually, Security and Intelligence." He had a badge in the palm of his hand and showed it to Skip, it was embossed with the initials DSS S&I. "Man Mountain, huh? Well, I've been called worse. The General asked me to keep an eye on things."

"So, you *were* a spy! Snooping in the files and casing the camp?"

"Not entirely. My son really *did* enjoy his week at camp, and for that I thank you. This was simply a fortunate coincidence. The General is very good at putting the right people into the right place at the right time." Otago looked at Skip for permission, then reached down to tug on the rope bindings. He nodded approval. "There was a rumor this guy had a buyer lined up for something worth millions. I was already scheduled to be here when he showed up. Then again, we also had to check out anyone who was spending time with the major."

"...with the major..." Skip paused. "Me?" he squeaked.

"Yes. You had a good recommendation, but we pride ourselves in a thorough background check." Otago motioned toward the back room. "Don't you think we should release your friend?"

Once Skip and Otago carefully cut the zip ties holding Chad to the chair, he pointed to the battered lockbox, now precariously hanging halfway off the wall. "Shouldn't we check to make sure Major Lukasz's *dilithium crystals* are safe?" Skip looked at him in shock. "Oh, now tell me you didn't think I'd figure it out. You know, Wilderness Counselor? I found the crash site the day after those 'movie props' arrived. I talked it over with him the last time you went into town—*and* I know you moved them from the admin building after the big guy over there was snooping around!"

Skip grimaced, then grinned as he reached into his pocket and pulled out the crystalline components from NIGHTFALL and placed them on the desk. "Actually, we don't have to. I really didn't like leaving them here without either Mike or I around. So, I pulled them out before we went to dinner tonight."

Otago laughed. "Nice." He pulled a radio off his belt and clicked the send button twice, then spoke. "All clear." Thirty seconds later, two men with military rifles slung on their backs came in the front door, looked at Otago, then headed toward the exam room after the master sergeant cocked his head in that direction. They returned with Lewis, still tangled, and roped, and headed out the front door.

Next into the room came Keith and Mike Lukasz. Otago came to attention and saluted, because Mike was in uniform. Otago picked up the NIGHTFALL components and waved them under Lukasz' nose. "Your chips, sir. You should probably take better care of them." He handed them to the officer.

Mike took the components and laughed. "Ah, but these are just decoys. The real ones are at Oak Ridge."

"But I saw you take them out of the..." Skip felt tired. He sat down in the chair where Chad had been tied up. In his tiredness, he'd almost blurted "...out of the X59." Yet even knowing that most of the people in the room probably knew the secret, he kept himself from saying it out loud. "I saw you put them in the lockbox."

Mike smiled. "Yes, I did, but I had several components that fried on re-entry. Smith and Jones brought me replacements. I kept the real ones on me and put defective parts into safekeeping. Hide in plain sight, remember? First you told me you thought someone was snooping, then Chad told me he saw the Sweathog out at the crash site, so I sent the real modules to Oak Ridge."

"When Chad told you...hmmm." Skip thought about that a moment. "...and you also knew about him?" He cocked a thumb over his shoulder toward Otago.

"Well, no, I didn't know General Thomas had sent the Master Sergeant until he called me tonight. As for your friends...Skip Davis, you know how to keep secrets, but you do not know how to be devious. It's a good thing you have smart friends who do." He put a hand up to forestall Davis' comment. "No, nothing you said gave it away. It still took Chad a while, even after he discovered the crash site."

"I *am* a wilderness counselor!" Chad responded proudly. "You're going to be a smart doctor, Skip, but up here in the mountains, we have to outthink city boys like you!" Chad apparently didn't think it was ironic to refer to himself as a local and Skip as a city boy. He looked more closely at his friend. "Maybe not so smart...Do you realize you've been burned?"

"Um. No?"

"He was fighting that fire even before I got there," said Keith. "So, he's probably got some smoke inhalation, too. Perhaps you'd best go into town and get checked out."

Chad nodded. "Give me your keys, City Boy! I'll drive you over to the hospital."

"Oh, like hell you will! Chad Jacobs, you've lived more years and in bigger cities than I have. You drive like a maniac...and you're not getting behind the wheel of my jeep!" Davis stood up quickly, then sat down even faster when his head started to swim. "Oh!" he said, then reached into his pocket and meekly handed the keys to Chad. Chad just grinned and took them.

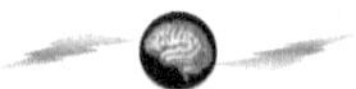

The final week went by quickly. Skip came back to work as assistant health officer since it was considered a "non-strenuous" job. The burn hadn't been too bad, but he developed a cough that took several days to get better. The doctor at the hospital had told him to limit strenuous activities for a few more days, so Skip continued at the Health Lodge even though Kesha was back. Mike stayed for the last week and continued to teach the Astronomy class. The aquatics staff, always the craziest of the bunch, had been painting themselves in blue body paint and running around pretending to be Venusians. Photography made their own home movie using some of the 'props.' Camper evaluations made it clear that the Space Movie Camp was their favorite theme and encouraged the staff to consider it for the whole following summer.

Next year.

"I won't be here next year," Skip told Mike. "Medical school is just too demanding. My camp days—at least until I have kids of my own—are pretty much ending tomorrow." The campers were leaving in the morning, and he knew *Heavy Lifter* was waiting at Oak Ridge to take Mike and NIGHTFALL out tomorrow night. The camp's volunteer service organization would come in to clean up the camp so that the everyone else could rejoin the twenty-second century. Regular staff would be leaving tomorrow afternoon.

As for next year's camp, there just wouldn't be time. Skip's parents were headed to Kauai next and wanted him to come to the Big Island during next summer's all-too-short break. Keith had offered to let him work just a few weeks, but Skip's fiancé Sara was thinking they should go ahead and schedule the wedding, since the break was too short for her to have Reserve duty. They'd get a brief honeymoon—in Hawaii! It was hard to argue with that plan.

Skip was stewing over decisions when Mike came into the Lodge with the day's mail. "S.C. There's someone here who would like to meet you." Mike stepped aside to reveal...the dark-suited man and woman from the airport and restaurant those many weeks ago. Only this time, the woman was not in a suit, but a military uniform with many badges and ribbons—and two stars on the collar. Skip was in shock, but Mike was grinning. "You'll need to learn to salute a general officer once you're an actual lieutenant, but you can be excused this time since you aren't in uniform yet. This is General Caroline Thomas. General, this is S.C. Davis, our new recruit."

Skip was speechless, only managing a stifled "—you..."

The general looked stern, with a piercing stare, but held out her hand. "Yes, Mr. Davis. Me."

Numbly shaking the general's hand, Skip forced himself to continue, "Um. Ma'am. Oh, yes, Ma'am. I, um...I thought you were a spy or something."

At this, General Thomas smiled and gave a friendly laugh. "I suppose I was, in a way, and you certainly had your share of those this summer. I flew out with Smith and Jones but instructed them to ignore me so I could look over the whole situation."

"Master Sergeant Otago said that 'The General' had sent him 'to keep an eye on things.'"

Thomas laughed. "Yes, Mr. Davis, although it seems the camp did a pretty good job themselves. After I got the report on your actions: glowing recommendations from Majors Donelly and Lukasz—plus Otago's 'not half-bad, I guess'—I figured I owed it to you to introduce myself." She handed Skip a thick envelope. "You need to read this, then I expect you'll have a phone call coming." She shook his hand once more, then turned and left.

Skip opened the envelope and started to read. His jaw dropped. He read it again, then finally looked up at Mike who was grinning.

The letterhead was a stylized representation of Earth and Mars, connected by a spiral. Underneath the logo it said: "Deep Space Survey Command, Office of Major Emerson Donelly, Ph.D., USSF, Training Liaison."

The text read:

"Mr. Simeon Case Davis:

"I am pleased to inform you that your application to the DSS has been accepted. You will be commissioned with the rank of Second Lieutenant in Space Force Reserve Officer Training until completion of your medical education."

The letter included additional pages detailing commissioning, responsibilities, confidentiality and something about 4th year med school rotations and residencies. It was signed by a Space Force general, then endorsed by 'Major General Caroline Thomas, US Army, Joint Survey Intelligence Command.' Up next to the letterhead was a hand-written note: "Conga-rats, Kay-det.—P.S. Ask Sara about her letter—Donnie." He went back to the first page of the letter and noticed with dismay a section that said he was required to report to Oak Ridge, Tennessee on Monday.

Monday? He would barely have time to go home, wash and repack. He had been torn between heading home to his apartment and seeing his aunt and uncle, versus staying on a few days to assist in camp shutdown. It was only a four-hour drive to Tennessee, but he had planned a small break before classes resumed. There wouldn't have been enough time to go see his parents, but at least Sara would be back at the end of the week.

Mike was grinning at him now, and Skip figured he must look like a fool, from the shock and then the disappointment. Of course, looks of shock and surprise had been his stock in trade all summer. Mike looked at him and said, "Don't worry, I have a feeling you'll enjoy Oak Ridge. There's a lot you need to learn, and it's better to get you started now. It won't be too bad."

Skip's phone rang.

"You'll want to take that, son, it's important."

"Hello?"

"Skip?"

"Sara!"

She sounded like she was out of breath. "I just came from the commander's office. I don't understand what's been happening, but I was so afraid something was wrong. Are you okay?"

"Sure, honey, it's been a bit busy. Sorry I haven't called, but you were supposed to be in drill." Skip looked up at Mike who had paused just inside the door. Mike winked at him and went outside.

"Oh, thank God! I was given orders to call you and then prepare to report to some army general by sixteen hundred tomorrow. They're going to put me on a suborbital in the morning to get there. I'm supposed to pack all my gear, report to this general in 'Lottie, and then I'm supposed to be on some special assignment in Oak Ridge for at least a week. I'm so afraid that this is going to ruin *all* our plans! I was told there was some big shake-up, and my name came up as perfect for the assignment. I knew I'd have to take whatever the Space Force assigned, but this is *too* much! I really don't understand why all of this happened so quickly."

It didn't seem like she had breathed at all, but she finally paused long enough for Skip to say something. "Honey, it's okay. I think a friend may have set us both up. I think we're going to manage to stay together."

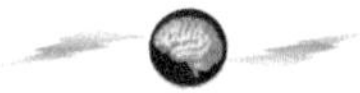

The fire had burned down to embers again. The boys had been very quiet during the tale and remained quiet for many moments to follow.

"Wow, Mister Davis, so you knew about the deep space missions before the rest of us! Did you go?" Ben asked.

"Naw, he's too old!" said one of the other boys, with the cocky assurance of youth. "Besides, my dad says the first ships to the outer planets were robots!"

"Well, sure, but the first *human* ships were sent by a group called DSS, right Mr. Davis?" Ben persisted.

"Oh, sure, but those are just campfire tales. You can only believe half of what anyone says around a campfire, right Miss Donelly?" said Davis with a wink at Donnie's grandniece.

S.C. Davis grabbed a sturdy branch, placed one end against his artificial leg and broke the branch in two to add it to the fire. He looked up at the sky with blurred vision, remembering triumph, disaster, lost and distant friends. But most of all he remembered that they had been first, no matter how much had been forgotten over the intervening years.

He cleared his throat and went on: "Now, let me tell you the one about The Lost Hand of Camp Runnamuck... "

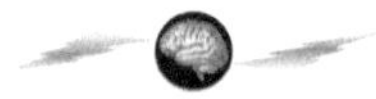

Acknowledgements

On A Starry Night was originally written in 2014 as a stand-alone novella. Unfortunately, plans to develop a series of "Campfire Tales" fell through, and the story sat for five years in a "completed but not published" folder on my computer. Then in 2019 I sold a short story to Chris Kennedy and Kevin Steverson in Kevin's *Salvage Title* universe. I've long thought that Kevin's stories have a similar feel to the old Time Machine stories by Donald and Keith Monroe ("Donald Keith") that appeared in *Boy's Life* when I was young. Talking with Chris one day, I happened to mention this story, and *he* happened to mention an open spot in Kevin's *The Long and the Short of It*. So, I sent the story to Kevin, and he liked it. We then figured out the (thankfully minimal) changes needed for it to fit his universe, and I got to fix some flaws that had bugged me in the original version.

It's been two years since that publication, and the wonders of indie publishing mean that I can now pursue my original plan of a series of novellas I once again call "Campfire Tales." Operation Nightfall has been modified to fit an ongoing series, so look for more to come from me and the friends I will invite along to play! I want to especially thank my sometimes co-author, sometimes co-editor, Sandra Medlock, for editorial assistance, as well as William Alan Webb and Jamie Ibson for cover and formatting assistance and advice. To the entire Peacemaker Cantina—I can't think of a better, more supportive, and more educational group of writers. To Kevin, thanks for a chance to play in your sandbox and find a first home for this tale. To Chris Kennedy, thanks for all of the opportunities.

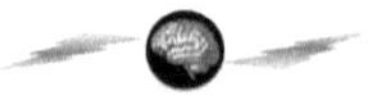

About the Author

Dr. Robert E. Hampson is a Neuroscientist and author. By day, he is a professor at Wake Forest School of Medicine, studying how our brains encode memory. By night, he writes military, adventure and hard-science Science Fiction as well as nonfiction articles explaining science to the general public.

Robert Hampson's SF writing career began with "They Also Serve," a short story in Riding the Red Horse, published in 2015. That story became the foundation of his first solo novel The Human Side, in 2020. He has three collaborative novels with Sandra Medlock, Chris Kennedy and Casey Moores in the "Wrogul's Oath" arc of the popular Four Horsemen Universe. A final book in this arc is expected in late 2023.

Rob's latest novel is *The Moon and the Desert,* an updated retelling of The Six Million Dollar Man. In addition to novels, he has co-edited two anthologies, and published more than 25 works of short fiction (some written as "Tedd Roberts"). He is also a regular contributor of nonfiction articles for science fiction readers, with more than 15 articles published. One of the articles, "Why Science is Never Settled," was nominated for the Hugo Award in 2015 as Best Related Work. Hampson has sequels in the works to both solo novels, the Wrogul's Oath, and The Founder Effect anthology.

Dr. Hampson's forty-year scientific career has ranged from studying the effects of commonly abused drugs on memory, to the effects of space radiation on the brain. His current work, as lead scientist for Braingrade, Inc., is developing a medical device to restore human memory function damaged by injury or disease. He is also a professor of physiology/pharmacology and neurology at

Wake Forest School of Medicine where he teaches regularly in the neuroscience and biomedical graduate curriculum. He also developed and teaches a course on Communicating Science, in which young scientists practice writing for—and speaking to—the general public. He is a scientific journal editor; a reviewer for dozens of journals and research agencies; has been interviewed on his research by newspapers, radio and TV; a consultant to TV and game producers, defense contractors, and authors. He has published more than 175 peer-reviewed scientific articles.

Hampson graduated in 1988 with a PhD from the Bowman Gray School of Medicine of Wake Forest University in Winston-Salem, NC. He has worked as a newspaper carrier, greeting card merchandizer, computer data entry operator and programmer, and laboratory technician, and lived in Pennsylvania, Texas, and North Carolina. He now lives in the Piedmont of North Carolina with his wife, Ruann.

Robert E. Hampson is available as a consultant through SIGMA — the Science Fiction Think Tank and the Science and Entertainment Exchange (a service of the National Academy of Sciences). His website is .

Books by Robert E. Hampson

The Moon and the Desert - Baen Books

ISBN 978-1-982192-49-5

What would it really take to make the Six Million Dollar Man? a medical thriller on earth and in space!

Glenn Armstrong Shepard had his sights set on going to Mars as a flight surgeon, but a training accident on the Moon left him crippled. Now he has a new plan: to be fitted with bionic prosthetics and come back even stronger.

Fate and the Space Force have other plans, and Glenn is grounded. Another doctor—his ex-fiancée—takes his place, and Glenn will have to fight to prove he can be an astronaut once more. . . .

The Human Side - Theogony Books

ISBN 978-1-648550-70-6

Is it an asteroid...or a weapon?

An asteroid headed toward Earth was not unexpected; multiple asteroids were a different story. And, when the "rock-throwing aliens" finally appeared, the people of Earth had to deal with a new type of war, where an enemy with powerful weapons held the high ground of space.

Dr. Tobias Greene felt guilty over patching up soldiers only to have them return to battle—until learning that his work was essential to the survival of the human race.

Master Sergeant Martin was a combat medic, trying to do his job and save as many as he could.

Lab Technician Kat Smith was forced out of her home and away from friends and family by the alien attacks. Her work was important, but would it be enough?

Jan and Li Janacek were trapped in New Mexico with their son, daughter, and eight other teens. They needed to get home...but home was no longer there.

For Arielle French, the aliens' arrival was everything she had predicted, until they attacked. Had she misunderstood their motives, or was it all the fault of the humans who failed to behave the way the aliens expected?

Technical breakthroughs might allow humans to resist the worst the "Rockers" could throw at them. But even if they could level the battlefield, though, would there be enough time left for Earth to show the Rockers what was really on the Human Side?

The Founder Effect - Anthology (edited with Sandra L. Medlock) - Baen Books

ISBN 978-1-982125-09-7

AWARD-WINNING AND BEST-SELLING AUTHORS CONTRIBUTE NEW STORIES: All-new fiction from Dragon Award winner and

New York Times best-selling author David Weber, Dragon Award nominee D .J. Butler, best seller Jody Lynn Nye, indie best sellers Chris Kennedy and Mark Wandrey, and more. Also featuring an introduction by multi-award-winning and New York Times best-selling author Larry Correia.

It is 2185 CE. Humans now live throughout the Solar System, but their most ambitious adventure is about to begin. The starship Victoria will carry over 10,000 colonists to a new world outside the Solar System. The larger-than-life exploits of those colonists will become legendary. The colonists will build a new civilization, and the actions of a few individuals will become famous—and infamous—forever marking their new colony with the Founder Effect.

Contributors: Larry Correia, Mark H. Wandrey, Les Johnson, Christopher L. Smith, David Weber, Daniel M. Hoyt, Brad R. Torgersen, Monalisa Foster, Sarah A. Hoyt, Chris Kennedy, Vivienne Raper, Jody Lynn Nye, Brent M. Roeder, Catherine L. Smith, Philip Wohlrab, D.J. Butler

Stellaris: People of the Stars - Anthology (edited with Les Johnson) - Baen Books

ISBN 978-1-481484-25-1

NEW STORIES AND ESSAYS FROM TOP AUTHORS AND EXPERT SCIENTISTS. Explorations of how interstellar travel may affect humanity by best-selling authors and scientists.

The stars will change us.

STELLARIS: PEOPLE OF THE STARS is a collection of original science fiction stories and nonfiction essays speculating about humanity's far-term expansion into the universe beyond the limits of our solar system—with an emphasis on the changes humans will undergo as a species as we make this happen. Is interstellar travel so far beyond our current imaginings that it will take a fundamental transformation of humanity in order to make it possible? And, if so, will we remain Homo sapiens or become a new and unique species—Homo stellaris (the People of the Stars)?

Herein are original science fiction stories by award-winning authors such as Kevin J. Anderson, William Ledbetter, Todd McCaffrey and Sarah A. Hoyt, supplemented by accessible nonfiction essays describing the science behind the fiction from people who should know—Sir Martin Rees (Astronomer Royal of the United Kingdom), Mark Shelhamer (Chief Scientist for the NASA's Human Research Program), and more.

This collection of original stories and essays was inspired by a gathering of scientists, science fiction authors, and futurists at a series of annual meetings held by the Tennessee Valley Interstellar Workshop. Let their speculations, imaginations and boundless sense of what's possible take your own journey beyond the edge of the solar system in STELLARIS: PEOPLE OF THE STARS!

Stories and Provocative Speculation from:

Sir Martin Rees, Kevin J. Anderson, Sarah A. Hoyt, Mike Massa, William Ledbetter, Todd McCaffrey, Kacey Ezell and Philip Wohlrab, Dan Hoyt, Les Johnson, Robert E. Hampson, Mark Shelhamer, Brent Roeder, Jim Beall, Cathe Smith

The Wrogul's Oath

Four Horsemen Universe

Books by Robert E. Hampson and Sandra L. Medlock

Do No Harm (Robert E. Hampson and Chris Kennedy with Sandra L. Medlock)

ISBN 978-1-950420-11-7

When Todd's critically damaged ship dropped out of hyperspace near the Human colony world of Azure, he had no memory of his past. He didn't know who he was, or even what he was, and the Humans didn't either. That didn't stop the colonists of Azure—they took him in, anyway...even though they didn't understand how he could do some of the things he could do.

Todd and his descendants consider themselves Human—eight armed and water-breathing—but Human, nonetheless. After seventy years living among Humans, Todd's descendants are going back out into the Union to make their mark—from fifteen-year-old Verne, who's a little short to be a mercenary, to Harryhausen, who wants to be the most famous PI in the galaxy. Eventually they learn that the rest of the Galactic Union knows them as Wrogul, intelligent octopus-like beings known for science and the ability to perform surgery like no other race can.

These Wrogul do more than just practice medicine, but they still intend to do no harm. Unfortunately, the Humans, whether they have two arms or eight, have powerful enemies... and the Wrogul may have no choice.

And Break It Not (Robert E. Hampson and Sandra L. Medlock)

ISBN 978-1-648551-92-5

The planet of Azure is nearly idyllic—there is a high standard of living, industry is booming, and the two races—Human and Wrogul—get along well with each other most days.

But underneath it all, there is tension between the races. Despite having no reason for it, the Humans don't always trust the Wrogul, and there is a faction within the Wrogul community that doesn't want its young growing up "Human."

When a large group of Wrogul move into the ocean and strange things begin happening—weird lights seen in the depths and sabotage at the mariculture stations—the Human's distrust becomes outright suspicion of treachery.

As things spiral out of control, another force enters the system—a group ostensibly sent by the UN on Earth to inspect the crops being grown on Azure—which threatens to destroy everything the Humans and Wrogul have worked for.

While the Wrogul still intend to do no harm, the Humans have powerful enemies in the galaxy, and, this time, the Wrogul may have no choice about whether to join the front lines with their Human friends. Will the threat of a common enemy break the relationship between the Humans and Wrogul...or break it not?

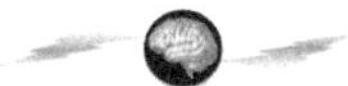

As My Witnesses (Sandra L. Medlock and Casey Moores with Robert E. Hampson)

ISBN 978-1-648554-17-9

Azure Colony avoided the larger conflicts of the Omega War and Guild Wars, only to fall prey to rogue mercenaries. Now they're rebuilding, but strange forces are at work. New friends on the ground and mysterious lights in the sky promise "interesting times" for the Humans and hyper-intelligent Wrogul of Azure.

Meanwhile, mercenary leader Verne and Peacemaker Harryhausen resume their search for the ancestral home of Azure's Wrogul. They encounter distrust, deceit, and misdirection from the all-powerful guilds, but they manage to learn of sightings of Wrogul-like aliens. Their strongest lead takes them to a forgotten system where a lost Human colony coexists with a strange alien race with remarkable similarities to the Wrogul.

But when they find the colony is in the middle of a civil war, they're forced to make a choice—do they choose sides or stand by while the colonists slaughter each other?

This I Swear (Sandra L. Medlock with Casey Moores and Robert E. Hampson)

Forthcoming in 2023 - the surprising conclusion to Todd's search for his ancestors.

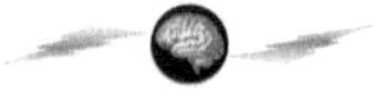

www.ingramcontent.com/pod-product-compliance
Lightning Source LLC
Chambersburg PA
CBHW021749190726
48290CB00008B/2554